Something
Terrible
Happened

A Richard Jackson Book

Something Terrible Happened

a novel by

Barbara Ann Porte

Orchard Books
New York

NORTH

This book is a work of fiction. Any similarities to real people, living or dead, are coincidental. Where real places have been named, they are used fictitiously.

Permission to quote from the following works is gratefully acknowledged. Page vii: "5.Green" from "The Colors of Night" from In the Presence of the Sun by N. Scott Momaday. Copyright © 1992 by N. Scott Momaday. Reprinted with permission from St. Martin's Press, Inc., New York, NY. Page 181: "Stopping by Woods on a Snowy Evening" from The Poetry of Robert Frost edited by Edward Connery Lathem. Copyright © 1969 by Henry Holt and Company. Reprinted with permission from Henry Holt and Company, New York, NY, and Jonathan Cape, London, England.

Orchard Books, 95 Madison Avenue, New York, NY 10016

Manufactured in the United States of America
Book design by Mina Greenstein
The text of this book is set in 12 point Simoncini Garamond.
10 9 8 7 6 5 4 3 2 1

Library of Congress Cataloging-in-Publication Data
Porte, Barbara Ann.
Something terrible happened : a novel / by Barbara Ann Porte.
p. cm.
"A Richard Jackson book"—T.p. verso.
Summary: Eleven-year-old Gillian is sent away from her mother who is dying of AIDS to live with her relatives in Tennessee.
ISBN 0-531-06869-2.   ISBN 0-531-08719-0 (lib.bdg.)
[1. Mothers and daughters—Fiction. 2. Death—
Fiction. 3. AIDS (Disease)—Fiction. 4. Afro-Americans—
Fiction.] I. Title. PZ7.P7995So 1994 [Fic]—dc20
94-6923

For Dima,
and Franklin

A young girl awoke one night and looked out into the moonlit meadow. There appeared to be a tree; but it was only an appearance; there was a shape made of smoke; but it was only an appearance; there was a tree.

—N. Scott Momaday,
"5. Green" from "The Colors of Night"

Contents

1

Gillian

DESPITE ANYTHING ELSE you may hear, this is the true story of what happened to Gillian starting that year. It is also about how something terrible can turn up in a family, any family, and change each family member's life forever. I sometimes picture them as standing in the path of an onrushing train, anyone helpless to stop it. Not that there is a train wreck in this story, but I believe the impact must have been similar. They would have been entirely unprepared. Especially Gillian, who had just turned ten, back then, when her world began unraveling.

I knew them all: Gillian, her mother, her whole family. Gillian's grandmother and I were friends in grade school. I wondered how she'd cope now; how her daughter would. I wondered most about Gillian.

I kept an eye on all three, listened for clues, stayed in touch. What I couldn't see, or didn't hear, I worked hard to imagine, and for more reasons than just loyalty. Shocking as it sounds, even to me, that's what I do. I'm a writer. I don't have to think twice when it comes to a story.

This was how Gillian looked that year: skinny, with long legs, a shy smile, and smooth gold-toned skin, the color a person could die for. Some people probably do—whitepeople who bake in the sun, risking cancer, hoping to get exactly that tan. Gillian's was natural. Natural, too, was her hair, down to her waist and nearly black, usually worn braided in one long plait down her back, twisted at the end. She didn't even need any rubber band to hold it in place. She had deep-set, dark chocolate eyes that always seemed to be taking in everything. If I had been asked at that age what I wanted to look like, I would have wanted to look like Gillian. There wasn't a thing wrong, yet, with her life either. She lived with her mother in a pleasant, sunny apartment with high ceilings, on Amsterdam Avenue—New York's Upper West Side, in case you're from somewhere else. Gillian's father was dead, but since she'd hardly known him, I think she couldn't have missed him that much.

"He died of a bad heart." That was how Gillian's grandmother explained his passing, why Gillian's mom was a widow, and why Gillian, almost as far back as she could remember, had no father. Gillian, listening carefully, had taken her grandmother's explanation literally; believed for years that it meant her father had been done in by his evil ways, the same as in old fairy tales.

I suppose in a way you could say he had been, but her grandmother only meant her son-in-law had died from a heart attack. It was easier than having to explain his bad habit, brought back with him from Vietnam. Certainly easier than recalling that one terrible night when he'd died in an ambulance on the way to the hospital, from a drug overdose.

It was on account of *that* war, was what they said among themselves, themselves being the people to whom they didn't have to bother telling the heart attack story. That was how, still listening carefully, Gillian learned the little she knew about her father who had once been a boy, a teenager, a college student who dropped out and was drafted, went to war, and came home with no visible wounds, but still shattered. It was two years later when Gillian was born.

By the time she was four, her father was gone. They say three's the borderline for memory. "If he'd only held on, I could have remembered more," Gillian used to say. As it was, she worked hard to recall even one or two things. She remembered a tall thin man, incredibly pale, with reddish hair falling over his face, swinging her high, and somebody screaming, herself screaming.

"You used to shriek with joy," her mother told her. "Then he'd swing you again into the air, heading for the ceiling, you reaching for the lights. 'More, more, more,' was the first thing you ever said. 'See, she's only a baby, but she's already talking in sentences.' Your daddy insisted on that."

"Did Daddy already look like a ghost then?" Gillian once asked. Her mother wrinkled her forehead. Then she laughed.

"Not a ghost. He was just an allwhiteperson, but color-blind. It was why he never wore ties. He couldn't tell if they matched." Gillian couldn't always tell, either, when her mother was joking.

Something else Gillian recalled from that time was this: "When my father lived with us, my mom was always shouting." But Gillian didn't know why; wasn't old enough to know. Afterward, her mother never shouted, did not believe in it, and also had no reason. While her husband was alive, she shouted against drugs and against needles.

"Shouted just to hear my own voice, for my own sake," she said. "I knew it was too late to change him. All that shouting was for me, to keep myself from changing. I wasn't about to become some wild woman like the ones you see everywhere on the streets all over this city, sharing drugs, sharing needles, sharing everything with anyone, including sharing their husbands and boyfriends." She was glad when she could stop shouting.

"Shouting can ruin your voice. An entertainer has to be careful. I don't plan to go on teaching forever. I see bright lights ahead." Gillian's mother had majored in theater in college. She still dreamed of life on the stage. But by then, of course, she had to earn a living. Luckily for her, she'd minored in education and was certified to teach high school English. This left her with time enough only for summer stock and weekend repertory. Even so, she guarded her voice, and why not? Sundays, when she sang in church, it sounded like an angel's.

"Dreams are like wings," she used to tell Gillian. "They can lift you so high."

"Dreams can make a person dizzy. We've always been practical people," Gillian's grandmother said. She meant not just herself and all Gillian's ancestors on her side. Oh, no. She meant to take in that whole sweep of people, Island people like themselves, who'd come north from warm sunny climates, paddling in boats, swimming, flying into airports; even women like these three, who had never so much as set foot on an island unless you want to count Manhattan, or possibly Long Island, or Staten.

"Sure, they came here following dreams," Gillian's grandmother told her. "But the first thing they did when they landed was get to work. Plus they never forgot who they were. Listen to me. I'm going to tell you a story." Gillian listened.

"ONCE THERE WERE two burros, a husband and a wife. They loved each other and lived together, very happy in the mountains, until a dry season came. No rain fell; no plants grew. There was nothing to eat and no water. 'We'll die for sure,' they told each other. They decided on a plan: to turn themselves into people, go looking for work. When the rains came again, they'd change back to burros, go home to the mountains, and live happily ever after. So that's what they did.

"The plan worked fine at first. They each found a job with a different farmer. The wife's farmer fell in love. He was mad for her. What could she do? In almost no time, they were married. They were living very well together when the rains came. Then, the burro turned man changed back to a burro, went home to the mountains to wait for his mate. But she didn't return. So he traveled from town to town, from farm to farm, crying out her name. Finally, he came to where she was living, making guava cakes in the kitchen for the farmer in the field. As soon as she heard her name being called, she dropped what she was doing. Right away, she started changing back—long ears, four legs, a tail bushing out from beneath her long skirt. 'I'm coming,' she brayed, and headed for the door.

"Just at that moment, however, the farmer returned from the field. He was looking forward to his tea and cake. How surprised he was to see a burro, fully dressed, exiting his house right through the front doorway, trotting down the walkway to where a second burro stood waiting. How hard that farmer stared as the two burros rubbed noses, kicked up their heels, and took off running. The farmer went inside to tell his wife. Of course, she wasn't there. He found only broken plates and pots, and guava paste stuck everywhere. So you can see how that was."

Gillian's grandmother ended her story.

"See how what was?" Gillian asked.

"See what can happen when you don't have a proper engagement. Falling in love isn't enough by a long shot. You want to know everything there is to know about your future spouse, including all about the in-laws—the brothers and sisters, uncles and aunts, the cousins, and especially the parents. Your mother fell in love just like that. Went off and got married. Don't you do that, Gillian," her grandmother warned her. "You see where it can lead."

Gillian was probably seven at the time. I think she

didn't have any plans to go off and get married. I wondered, though, when I first heard that story, what about the children? Couldn't *they* choose better, too, if before they were born they already knew everything there was to know about their parents? But of course, children don't get to choose. Anyway, if you'd asked Gillian then, she would have told you, no one could have chosen a better mother than hers.

2

Island Women

THAT'S WHAT Gillian thought, and I thought so, too. Almost anyone seeing those two together would have thought it. I close my eyes and see them even now: mother and daughter strolling happily along a city street, window-shopping, holding hands, eating hot roasted chestnuts from a brown paper bag, unthinking of danger. They call to mind that old Greek myth, the boundless love of Demeter and her only child, Persephone. Gillian and her mother even looked as I imagine those two did—dark-eyed and regal, with a richness of hair, and an air about them as vibrant as springtime. No wonder strangers turned to stare. To tell the truth, strangers stared anyway, even when Gillian wasn't there. No one I knew was more stylish or better dressed than Gillian's mother or, for that matter, her grandmother, too.

"Island women dress well," Gillian's grandmother liked to say, sitting at the kitchen table, straightening some seam, taking a tuck, pinning up a skirt. "Everyone knows it. Late every afternoon, unless it is raining, all over the Islands women put on fancy straw hats, pull up white gloves, walk to the center of town to have tea."

"What women?" Gillian asked. "How come in all the pictures I see, people are wearing bikinis? Hardly even that."

"Ah," her grandmother answered. "But those are tourists. It is only visitor information propaganda, aimed at these United States. Americans are so gullible."

That Gillian's mother and grandmother could dress as they did—have their hair styled, their shoes heeled, their hose perfect—on just a teacher's salary, after all, in her grandmother's case a social worker's, was close to amazing. They knew how to shop, picking up this or that belt, purse, or scarf in one thrift store or another, making their rounds in the most fashionable sections of the city. VINTAGE BOUTIQUES read the door signs. "Downtown you're wasting your time," they told each other. They saw to it Gillian dressed well, too. It helped that they knew how to sew, and I don't mean just mending. There was that wonderful coat, for instance, Gillian's mother made her one Christmas, I think the year she turned eight.

Gillian was so proud of it. She wore it everywhere. It was of the softest red wool, so red you blinked the first time you saw it. It had wide cuffs, a cowl-shaped hood, and a sturdy brass zipper up the front. *Go ahead, wind, just try to get through,* Gillian's mom must have thought, sewing. That coat was warm, for sure, but warm wasn't what made it special. Appliquéd on the back in black felt was a large map of Africa and also parts of the Mediterranean and the Arabian peninsula. Country names were embroidered in silk; red and green threads, violet, and yellow, and blue. To the east, under Gillian's right arm, lay part of India. The Atlantic Ocean wound around to her left; and spilled across the front was the Caribbean Sea, with so many small islands, and most of their names: Cuba, the Bahamas, Jamaica, Haiti, Dominican Republic, Puerto Rico, St. Croix, St. Martin, Antigua, Montserrat, Guadeloupe, Dominica, Martinique, St. Lucia, Barbados, Trinidad and Tobago. The northern edge of South America was pictured—Suriname and Guyana, parts of Venezuela and Colombia. The southernmost tip of Florida rested near Gillian's right shoulder, with a tiny arrow pointing north.

"Gillian's coat of arms," her grandmother called it, and meant that it was almost like a family tree. It was certainly extraordinary, and the first time Gillian put it on, her mother took her to visit her great-grandmother, who lived in White Plains, to show off the sewing. She borrowed a car for the trip. Gillian's grandmother went along for the ride.

"That's some coat, Gillian," said Gigi-ma, the name by which Gillian called her, it being a private abbreviation. Gigi-ma peered through thick metal-rimmed eyeglasses and examined the coat inside and out. She admired the lining and stitching. "Nice work," she finally told Gillian's mom, having been the one who'd first taught her to sew and embroider. Gigi-ma leaned back in her chair then, but her eyes lingered on the Islands. "I could have used a coat like that on the boat to New York with my mom. We all could have. That was one cold trip, believe me," she said.

Gillian had heard it before, but she liked hearing once more how her great-grandmother had left Trinidad at age three with her sister and mother, how they'd arrived in New York Harbor on the coldest day of the decade, with only the clothes on their backs and what they could carry. "It was so cold, I thought we'd never be warm again," Gigi-ma said every time. "I would have turned right around that minute and gone back home if I could. Of course I couldn't. I was only three. But my mother couldn't either."

"Why couldn't she?"

"She couldn't because she couldn't. Didn't I just say so?" was Gigi-ma's only answer. "Besides, she wouldn't have anyway. 'Never look back. Always look ahead' was her motto.''

Gigi-ma could have said more. Young as she was at the time, she still remembered how they hurried. The reasons they did, she knew secondhand, pieced together from conversations her own mother had held through the years in the kitchen. Listening was how Gigi-ma knew about the strikes and the riots, the outbreak of fires that year; and about how her father was killed. He was in the real estate business. He'd gone to inspect what was left of a house after a blaze. A rafter broke, and the roof collapsed. He died on the spot, and so did two workmen. That was when Gigi-ma's mother packed their belongings, just what they could carry, took both her children, locked up her house, kissed her parents good-bye, and boarded the next boat leaving for New York. "It wasn't hard to see the writing on the wall. We didn't get out a moment too soon, believe me," Gigi-ma's mother said afterward. Gigi-ma believed her, but hard as she tried, she could never recall more than one or two things from before the trip.

"Don't ask me anything about that Island," she usually said if her child, or grandchild, or great-grand-child did. "I was too young to remember. I remember New York, icy cold winters, a brownstone apartment in Brooklyn, dresses so starched they almost stood by themselves, nuns who wore habits in Catholic school, prize roosters kept by some neighbors for fighting, collecting rents with my mother, who managed other people's properties. Real estate was the only business she knew." On that day when Gillian came to visit, though, Gigi-ma read the names of the Islands on the coat, and her memory was refreshed.

"Such beautiful Islands," she said. "Beautiful mountains, beautiful beaches, beautiful forests. So much sunshine. It was never cold. Warm rains fell in summertime. The trees were so tall, so big around, the flowers so bright—you can't begin to imagine. So many kinds of birds, so many colors. Even the butterflies were breathtaking. Island people had such good manners. 'Good morning. Good evening. How is your family?' Strangers stopped in the street to pass the time of day."

"So why did you leave?" Gillian asked. "Why did your mother leave such a beautiful Island to come to New York?" Gillian's great-grandmother looked surprised by the question.

"I guess for the same reason people usually do, day after day, month after month, year after year," she finally said. "Something terrible happens; then you leave, heading someplace else, hoping for the best."

"What terrible thing?" Gillian wanted to know. But Gigi-ma didn't answer. She'd fallen fast asleep.

"Getting old," Gillian's mother said.

"WHAT TERRIBLE THING? Where was Gigi-ma's father? Why didn't he come, too?" Gillian asked, going home.

"He was already dead," her grandmother said. "They left on account of some fire."

Maybe Gigi-ma's father burned up in the flames, Gillian thought. That would have been terrible. No wonder no one ever talked about it.

3

A Love Story

EVEN AFTER Gillian was too old to need "tucking in" anymore, her mother still liked to come into her room at night, sit on her bed, and tell stories. This was a favorite of both of theirs:

AGES AGO, a widowed mother and her daughter followed a parrot over mountains and deserts, across half a world, in search of a wonderful fruit the bird knew about that grew only on a certain tree in the center of the rain forest. After finding and eating the fruit, the mother was very thirsty. She asked her daughter please to make a leaf cup and fetch water from the stream. No sooner was the daughter gone, however, than a tiger appeared and ate up the mother. As she was dying, she sang this song:

"Daughter, dear daughter,
Don't weep for me when I'm gone;
Wherever you go, my spirit will follow,
A mother's love is that strong."

The daughter heard the song as she was re-
turning with the water. Where her mother had
been, she found only a pile of bones and some hair.
Then she heard the tiger growl. The girl climbed
the nearest tree and stayed there, hidden among its
branches, for seven nights and seven days, with no
food or water except for the fruit that grew on the
tree. On the seventh day, a cowherd passed, saw
her, and persuaded her to come down. Soon after,
they were married. Seasons came and went. A little
girl was born.

Now, the daughter had carried her mother's
bones and hair back from the forest and buried
them beside the house. From this place, a snake-
gourd plant had sprouted. The little girl made herself a lute from one of its dried-up gourds. Whenever she played this instrument, her mother seemed
to hear the song *her* mother had sung as she was dying, and she felt sure her mother's spirit was
nearby.

Time passed. The little girl was old enough to
go to school. Her father still herded cows, and her
mother took a part-time job in town. How sur-

prised the mother was coming home every day to find the housework had been done. She couldn't understand what was happening. She made up her mind to find out.

The next day, when her husband and little girl were leaving, she, too, started out for work as usual. But soon she turned around, came back, and hid behind a tree outside her kitchen window. You can imagine her amazement when she saw a woman step out from the snake-gourd lute and begin tidying the house. She could tell right away the woman was her mother. The daughter rushed in and embraced her. "Don't you ever go away and leave me again!"

"Of course not," said her mother. "Do you know how much trouble it took getting back?" When the daughter's husband and little girl returned home, they also rejoiced, and everyone lived happily ever after.

"Which goes to show how strong a mother's love can be for her daughter," Gillian's mother said every time she came to the end of this story. Gillian never grew tired of hearing it. Sometimes, though, she did wonder about fathers and why they so seldom appeared in her mother's stories. Finally, she asked.

"How come your stories are never about fathers?"

"Never?" said her mother, incredulous.

"Almost never," said Gillian. Whatever the reason, her mother's practice seemed contagious. As Gillian grew up, she concentrated on mothers and daughters, too. Here's an example. Gillian wrote it for school.

First the cover: GILLIAN KAMEESHA HARDWICK, AN AUTOBIOGRAPHY is printed in heavy black crayon letters on red construction paper. Below is a drawing of a tall, slim, light brown woman, her head wrapped in an emerald turban. Everything about her looks elongated, including her huge dark eyes; her nose; and her ears, from which dangle a pair of gold earrings. She's dressed like a dancer in a yellow leotard, a waltz-length turquoise skirt, and white toe shoes that lace up her legs. Beside her stands a long-necked, long-armed, long-legged child, with a thick, dark braid pulled forward over one shoulder and twisted at its end. She resembles the woman, except her coloring is lighter, and the earrings she wears are tiny hoops that do not dangle. Though she is dressed in a red-and-white-striped T-shirt, blue jeans, and sneakers, with her stance she, too, could pass for a dancer. Alongside her stands a plain wooden folding table with a glass bowl on top containing a goldfish.

Gillian's composition is written neatly in cursive with a ballpoint pen on white, blue-lined paper.

I, Gillian, am nine years old. I was born in New York City. I live with my mother and a goldfish named Josephine. We are very cozy in our apartment. My mother and I go to school every weekday and come home together. I am in fourth grade. My mother teaches English in high school. She is also an actress and singer on weekends. Sometimes, she sings solo in church. Then I sing in the choir. When she is in a play, I get to watch the rehearsals. Sometimes, I sit in the audience on opening night. Other times, I spend weekends with my grandmother in Queens. Josephine keeps my mom company. We are West Indian. My grandmother's mother came to this country on a boat from Trinidad when she was three. My mother and I are very happy together. Our goldfish is happy, too. Happily ever after. The end.

As anyone can tell, reading this, nothing terrible had happened yet. There wasn't even a hint of trouble ahead. In fourth grade, it was still possible to believe in happy endings.

On the other hand, a person might wonder, wouldn't a father in the house have been better? Possibly, but there's also this to consider: a father, however wonderful he may be, however kind and beloved, still needs attention. He has to be fed, watched over, worried about. No matter how loving a father is, he will always be a distraction.

Gillian's mother had only Gillian to worry about. "See, it's just the two of us, so I can indulge her." They went everywhere, did everything, together. They shopped for clothes and groceries, went to church, concerts, restaurants, visited friends, cooked, cleaned, did laundry, sometimes even bathed together. Long, steamy hot baths late at night, with bubbles and bath salts, soaping each other's back, rinsing each other's hair with lemon juice, rosemary, honey.

Did I say *everything*? Almost everything. Because don't you know there were times when Gillian's mom, like any mom, felt the need for grown-up company, conversation that didn't include a child, even her own—someone her own age to giggle or cry with. Don't you know, sometimes she wanted this, too, a man's arms wrapped around her, reminding her she was a woman as well as a mother. Those times, she'd take Gillian to her grandmother's and leave her there overnight. "I've got late rehearsals," she'd say.

Gillian didn't mind. Why would she? She loved her mother, but she also loved her grandmother. They ate out together: Chinese, East Indian, Ethiopian foods. They ate in, too; her grandmother cooked Island foods, curried stews, seafood creole, fried plantains, callaloo soup. They went to movies, museums, botanical gardens. They visited Gillian's great-great-aunt Sylvia, who lived nearby, Gigi-ma's younger sister who'd come here on the boat as an infant, carried in her mother's arms. Aunt Sylvia had only one arm, the left one.

"What happened to her right arm?" Naturally, Gillian wanted to know.

"She lost it in an accident," her grandmother told her.

"What sort of accident?" Gillian asked.

But her grandmother only said, "Please, it was a long time ago," as though that were an answer. Therefore, for some time to come, Gillian listened more closely than ever to kitchen conversations that didn't concern her, and found out.

"A woman on her own can't be too careful. Ask me. I know," Gillian heard her great-great-aunt Sylvia say to her grandmother. "My mother knew best, and I'm sure you do, too." They were discussing Gillian's mom and gentlemen friends. They didn't stop there. "See, if I'd listened to *my* mother instead of running around with a wild man, I wouldn't have lost my right arm to his machete. But I was pretty wild myself when I was young."

A machete? Gillian was astounded. It was not the sort of accident that had ever crossed her mind. She had trouble, too, picturing this aunt, so plump and even-tempered now, once young and wild.

"What sort of accident did Aunt Sylvia have with

her boyfriend's machete?" Gillian asked her grandmother later.

Her grandmother looked at her sharply, then said, "Running wild was the accident. A jealous man is always bad news. Gigi-ma and my grandmother warned her. He came after her with his machete because he thought she had another boyfriend on the side."

"Then what happened?" Gillian asked. She meant what happened to the man.

"Nothing," her grandmother said. "In those days, the police didn't care to get involved in what they called Island matters. All things considered, it could have turned out worse."

"Well, sure. She could have been dead," Gillian said.

"Right, that too," said her grandmother. "But what I had in mind was, afterward the man decided a one-armed girlfriend wasn't for him, and he left Aunt Sylvia alone. Still, he felt so bad for what he'd done, he wanted to make it up to her. At that time, my grandmother owned a part interest in a bakery. Aunt Sylvia and Gigi-ma ran it. It's hard making bread with only one arm. He paid for Aunt Sylvia to go back to school. She studied accounting, a job that doesn't take two hands to do. That's how Aunt Sylvia became the first person in our family to get a college degree in this country."

"I see," said Gillian, though she really didn't. Several weeks later the subject came up in school, in geography. There was a picture in a textbook of a machete. *A large, heavy-bladed knife used for cutting sugarcane* read the caption. Gillian raised her hand.

"Yes, Gillian?" the teacher said.

"Nothing. I forget," Gillian stammered. She could hardly believe she'd been about to say, "Years ago, my great-great-aunt had her right arm chopped off by a jealous man swinging a machete." What would the teacher have thought of this family?

Instead, the next month, when Gillian had to write a composition for class about a relative who wasn't a parent or grandparent, she wrote:

My great-great-aunt Sylvia came here on a boat when she was a baby. She has only one arm. She lost the other in an accident. She used to be a baker, but now she is a retired accountant. I like visiting her with my grandmother. She always has good things to eat: fried red beans, coconut milk, tamarind, dried papaya. She's also a collector: seashells, clay whistles, carved animals, music boxes, colored minerals and stones. She gave me a pink rock one time to take home.

This was all true, but not the whole story.

"What's that you've got in your pocket?" Gillian's

grandmother asked her once, when they were leaving. Her grandmother was helping her button her coat.

"I don't know," said Gillian, looking surprised.

"Rose quartz," Aunt Sylvia said informatively, as Gillian's grandmother held up the stone. "It came from the Islands."

"I wonder how it got into my pocket," said Gillian.

"I wonder, too," said her grandmother.

"Probably fell," said Aunt Sylvia. "You'd better keep it. I'm too old to have much use for a lucky stone like that."

Gillian left this part out of her composition. She didn't want her family to sound superstitious. She also didn't want her teacher to think she was unreliable. A lucky stone, after all, falling into her pocket. Of course, had Gillian thought enough about it, truly thought about it, she might have wondered what sort of luck a stone could bring, lifted from a one-armed woman who'd lost her other arm to a machete. But then, Gillian wasn't superstitious.

4

The Strongest Mother in the World

GILLIAN'S MOTHER wasn't superstitious either. Even so, the winter when Gillian was ten, her mother lay in a hospital bed, hoping for a miracle. Gillian and her grandmother hoped for one, too.

Gillian's mother had been brought to the hospital by ambulance, been taken straight to emergency after having collapsed in the street. There'd been earlier signs, vague symptoms—an intermittent cough and fatigue. She'd gulped down more vitamins, eaten more vegetables. She'd made the rounds of doctors, some of them specialists in their fields. It's hard to imagine, almost impossible to believe, but none of them ever tested her for AIDS, acquired immune deficiency syndrome, or even mentioned the possibility. Why didn't they? And what about Gillian's mother? Was she afraid? Did she think just to name something also could cause it? Or did she believe what she said later: "I'm a good person. I've always been a good daughter. I eat right, go to church, work hard, take good care of Gillian. This can't be happening to me."

"Sorry to have to do this to you," white-coated technicians in double rubber gloves told Gillian's mother each time they explored to find a usable vein, inserted a needle, took more blood.

"We're trying to assess the damage to your system," her doctor, a pulmonary specialist, explained. He, and everyone approaching her, did so with extraordinary caution and exquisite kindness; as one might treat the recently bereaved, or someone maybe just about to be. Like Gillian, for instance.

Not that she'd yet grasped the full situation, and why would she, when visitors to that room all so carefully denied it.

"We thought we'd lost you for sure, but see, you pulled through."

"God is looking out for you, girl."

It was as though not one of them had ever heard of AIDS until that minute; had no idea, none whatsoever, that AIDS was a fatal disease.

"Doctors don't know everything," they told each other. "Hey, they don't really know *anything* about AIDS." Well they did know one thing. Everyone who got it eventually died. It was just a matter of time.

"Shoot, we all die eventually, don't we?" they said, trying hard to look only on the bright side. They told each other good-news stories. Everybody knew somebody who had some terrible condition but was defeating all odds. Or else knew *of* somebody: that famous scientist, for instance, with Lou Gehrig's disease; someone's lawyer cousin with multiple sclerosis; a musician past middle age with cystic fibrosis; all of them going to work, getting by.

"It's like I heard somebody saying on television. You've got to keep a positive attitude." Gillian's grandmother certainly did.

"See, she's improving every day. She's put on weight. Her color's better. My child is going to live." Gillian's grandmother said it over and over, as if her daughter's life depended on it. She asked the opinion of everyone she knew.

Mine went like this: it's always a fine line between a positive attitude and acceptance of what will be. But this was what I told her: "One day, someone with AIDS is going to live. Why shouldn't it be your child?"

"The main thing when your mother comes home from the hospital is not to wear her out," Gillian's grandmother told Gillian. "We don't want her to worry. We have to make sure she eats right, takes vitamins, gets plenty of rest. She's always been healthy, been strong. You'll see, in no time at all she'll be better, fully recovered, back on her feet." Gillian's grandmother had moved in with Gillian while her mother was gone, so that Gillian would not have to miss too much school. They both heard a lot of advice.

"Proper nutrition is the main thing," said some, and provided lists of nutrients and recipes.

"The main thing is trusting in God," said others, and offered their prayers.

"You want to keep on top of the latest research," instructed informational brochures.

"You want the best medical care," the pulmonary specialist advised.

"Don't overlook old-time cures either," still others told them, and passed along names of practitioners they knew who dealt in roots and herbs.

Gillian's approach was direct; she made deals with God, or tried to: "Let my mother live, and I'll be good from now on." Gillian remembered every bad thing she'd ever done, and confessed it, promised never to do it again: not talk back, not dawdle coming home from school, not forget to do her homework, not neglect to clean her room or do the dishes; not even *think* about taking anything that wasn't hers, a lucky stone, for instance. Gillian fingered the one from Aunt Sylvia. "I'll never do anything bad so long as I live."

Of course, that's not possible. And even if it were,

it wouldn't work. That's what Youseff, her best friend in Sunday school, told her.

"Would too," she said.

"Would not," he said back, and set out to prove it. "Wasn't Jesus good, as good can be? But see, even being God, being the Son of God, being that good, didn't save Him from dying. How you think it's gonna save someone else?"

Gillian spoiled being good right that second. She swung back her fist, hit Youseff in the face. That evening, her grandmother sent her to her room to think about her behavior. She used the time to catch up on homework, an overdue assignment: fifth-grade folklore unit—make up a modern fairy tale or a fable.

Ages ago, a girl and her mother lived together and were happy. They were also good. Well, they tried to be. Now and then, hardly ever, the little girl's mother forgot—ate the wrong foods, didn't get enough sleep, stayed away too long on a weekend. No wonder she got sick. Nobody knew what was wrong with her, though, or how to make her well.

One night, the little girl dreamed that if her mother could have a certain kind of fruit that grew on a certain tree in the middle of the rain forest, she would get better. There was only one rule. The fruit had to be picked by a person who was always good, which the little girl was. That's why, the next morning, she packed some lunch and a change of clothes and set out to find it. She crossed mountains and deserts, traveled over an ocean, until she came to the ends of the earth, and there was the rain forest. In the very densest part stood a beautiful tree with green leaves and wonderful fruit growing at the top. The little girl climbed the tree and picked just enough fruit to make three dinners. Then she climbed down, traveled back over the ocean, crossed deserts and mountains, and fed the fruit to her mother. Her mother got better. Afterward, she always ate right, got plenty of sleep, and stayed home every weekend. She never got sick again.

Sometime later, that little girl's mother said to her, "It was very good of you to go to all that trouble to get me some fruit, but, see, I would have gotten better anyway. Don't worry. I would never go away and leave you. I love you much too much, and, also, women in my family live almost forever."

The little girl knew that was true. Her great-grandmother was already very old, and HER mother had lived into her hundreds. Then the little girl understood, and didn't worry anymore. She knew she had the strongest mother in the world and that her mother would always be with her. But just in case, the little girl made up her mind to keep on being good; and she was, always. Happily ever after. The end.

Gillian got an *A*, and why not? It was a good story, properly punctuated for the most part, and it certainly sounded like a fairy tale.

5

A Queen Seeking Cures

IT WAS almost the start of summer vacation when Gillian's mother finally came home from the hospital. She was a changed woman, a different person. She was out of her head, maybe just beside herself with grief. Anyone could tell simply by looking or by listening. Neighbors knew it right away, seeing her on the street, in the hallways, talking to herself, draped in bright parrot-colored clothes, her head elaborately wrapped in rich African cloths, her feet always in sandals. She wore bangles on her wrists and long showy earrings. She strapped bells onto her ankles. She jinglejangled whenever she moved. She moved very carefully, holding herself painfully straight, stiff-limbed, as though to let down her guard for one minute would risk her breaking into pieces.

"She's crazy. Lost her mind in that hospital," some people said.

"It could be just temporary. Hospitals can do that to you," said others. But see what it was, AIDS can do that to you; go straight to the head, affect the brain, make a person act strange.

"She's fine when she gets enough rest, takes her vitamins. 'You have to eat regular meals,' I tell her. 'Plenty of fruit and vegetables. Drink at least three glasses of carrot juice daily, and plenty of ginger tea.' She's okay when she listens to me." That was Gillian's grandmother talking, to whomever.

"She's scared. That's what your mother is," Gillian's mother's latest boyfriend told Gillian the day they both went together to be HIV tested. The tests came back negative a few weeks after. "Good luck. You be good now, hear, and take care of your mom," the boyfriend said to Gillian. He kissed her good-bye on the top of her head and disappeared.

"He's just scared," Gillian's grandmother said. "I never knew a man to be there when you needed him." Well, her experience was limited. Surely, though, Gillian was scared, too. She had no experience preparing her to deal with a mother who was grieving for herself, desperate for a cure; who clutched at any straw and claimed every day that she was royalty.

"I'm a queen," she told Gillian. "You are a princess. We are all queens and princesses. All of us who are good." Day by day, Gillian's mother grew thinner and frailer. Strangers held open doors, gave up their seats on the buses, even carried packages for her. "See, they can tell I'm a queen just by looking," she said. And all that seething hot summer, she and Gillian traipsed through the city, tracking down cures, rumors of them.

First there was the medicine prescribed by the hospital: experimental pills, blood thinner, antibiotics, medicine to prevent seizures, pills to help her over feeling sick from all the other pills.

"How can medicine make me better when it makes me too nauseous to eat?" she asked. Most days she skipped some. She substituted strong-smelling herbal teas and broths steeped with twisted roots and bark, hard to find, even in this city, and expensive. She and Gillian took buses; later she sent Gillian alone, uptown and downtown, to the East and West Sides, down flights of stairs to damp basements, up flights of stairs to dark apartments, where smooth-skinned West Indian women, African women with scars on their cheeks, a family of Romanian Gypsies mixed powders and tonics and called themselves in business.

Dr. Chin, whose ground-floor home was also her office, told Gillian, "The human body is like a small world. It needs to be in harmony with nature. Summer is for growth; now is a good time to start treatment." She showed her a huge leather-bound book of ancient prescriptions. The writing was Chinese, black ink characters on paper yellowed from age. Pictures were on every page: plants, animals, minerals. "See, we use all these things." She named some: ginseng, myrtle, dandelion, cinnamon, fenugreek, turmeric, rhubarb, senna, indigo, tooth of a panda, horn of a deer.

Gillian watched as Dr. Chin crushed leaves, sliced roots and bark, ground powders with a pestle in a large marble bowl or in a cast-iron mortar. She added milk, sometimes lard; folded the medicines in papers or put them in capsules; gave them to Gillian with written instructions about which ones to boil and when to take them. She believed in exercise, too. The only wall in her prescribing room not lined with wooden drawers and locked glass-door cases contained a chart showing Chinese people in red and black robes, bending and bobbing. "Forty separate movements to cure and prevent diseases," Dr. Chin said, and instructed Gillian on how to instruct her mother in bending, stretching, pretending to be a tiger, a bear, a deer, an ape, and a crane.

"Chinese medicine is thousands of years old," Gillian told her mother and grandmother hopefully.

"Yes, I know," her grandmother said, but sounded doubtful. Even so, she herself sent money to Mexico for an expensive tonic. "It makes the cells replace themselves faster," she said. The tonic came in glass vials, each one a dose, to be taken four times a day. She lined up the vials in glasses of ice water in the refrigerator. "If it isn't kept cold, it won't work. When the ice melts, it's your job to add more, and also to make sure your mother takes it on time," she told Gillian.

Gillian worried. She knew such kinds of medicine worked slowly. What if her mother didn't have enough time? Every day she looked worse, thinner and weaker. Once a morning person, now she regularly slept past noon.

"It's after lunch," Gillian would say anxiously, nudging her mother's bony shoulder underneath the blankets. "Wake up!" Then her mother would sit up in bed and stretch like a crane.

"What's the hurry? As long as we're up before the banks close, we're on time, isn't that so, Gillian?" she'd ask, giggling.

They went to the bank frequently, and withdrew money to pay for the medicines. On their way home, they usually stopped to eat out, often in Ethiopian restaurants. "See, this kind of food is just what I need," Gillian's mom would say, ordering collard greens and goat stew, leaving most of it on her plate. She had sores in her mouth and her throat was dry. Whole days went by when she couldn't swallow, but she tried. She broke off pieces of flat white bread and dipped them into gravy. "No utensils, only our hands.

Our hands are clean, no germs," she said. "So much more sanitary than silverware. Germs are why so many people are dying." She washed herself constantly: her hands, her face, her hair, her whole body. "A queen has to keep clean," she said.

Gillian no longer bathed with her. The water was too hot, too salty, too oily, too brown or too green with special muds and clays and other additives, all said to be therapeutic. The steam was so thick with herbal fragrances it was a wonder anybody could breathe in that bathroom. Gillian didn't try, except when her mother needed her help. Other times she lay in her bed, covered her head with a pillow, wanting to block out the sounds of hymns her mother was singing in tones more haunting and beautiful than ever. Listening could break a person's heart.

"What will become of me, Gillian?" her mother once asked toward the end of summer, sitting on Gillian's bed after a bath. "I worry for my mother. Will I soon weigh sixty pounds and need her to feed and change me like a baby? Gillian, what are we to do?"

"Don't worry," Gillian told her. "You'll get better. You're getting better already. I'll always take care of you." But afterward, alone in her bed, Gillian wept. What *would* become of them? What would become of her? I wondered that, too.

THERE WAS a path, and everyone who took it died. What killed them was unknown, but wherever it went soon there was the sound of weeping and wailing.

Old stories come back to haunt us. Find one cure, and something else starts hurting. Queens don't just lie back and die, though, thought Gillian's mother.

It was September when she snatched her child from her mother's house, right out from under her own mother's nose. She walked alone into that apartment one Saturday morning and walked away with Gillian.

"What could I do? It's her child, after all," said Gillian's grandmother. She had brought Gillian home with her the week before, enrolled her in public school there. "Just until your mother starts feeling better," she told her. Out of Gillian's hearing, she said, "The child can't stay in *that* city." She meant Manhattan's Upper West Side. "There's crack on the streets, too many guns, so much crime. Someone has to look after her properly, see to it she's going to school. Her mother's too sick, and I'm not living close enough by."

Going to school wasn't a problem for Gillian's mom. She'd lost her job, been fired. It gave her time to travel.

"They can't fire a person for being sick, can they? Isn't it against the law?" I asked that the first time I heard of it.

"Go fight city hall! See how far you get," was the answer.

Gillian and her mom got as far as Florida.

"There's a place down there where I can be cured," her mom told her. They traveled by bus. It's not hard to picture: one tall, emaciated woman; one worried-looking child. The woman is barelegged, in sandals; long, gathered folds of brilliant gold material cascade from her shoulders to her ankles; and wound around and around her head, covering her hair completely, is a shimmering strip of chartreuse silk. Another passenger brushes by, hand touching hand, and pulls back, alarmed that any living skin could be so hot and dry. But it is Gillian's mother's eyes that attract the most attention, dark and vigilant, glittery with fever. Beside her, Gillian seems almost nondescript, neatly dressed in T-shirt, jeans, and sneakers; her hair combed back and plainly braided. But then I think again, and I'm struck by their elegance, their grace under pressure: those long long necks, their heads held high, that posture. Why not believe Gillian's mother's claim to royalty, believe at least that they are descended from it?

"Queens don't carry much luggage," Gillian's mother told her, putting Gillian in charge of the single, medium-sized valise they had between them. It contained a week's change of underwear for each, T-shirts and jeans and a light summer outfit or two for Gillian, and lengths of bright cotton for her mother. What was she thinking of? Winter was coming. Already, she often felt chilled. I'd guess that being sick had made her gullible, not just about cures but also about Florida weather. She herself was encumbered by only one item, a knotted white pillowcase, whose gathered ends she gripped in one fist.

"Sssh, it's our treasure," she told Gillian in a whisper, giggling, crossing her lips with one long index finger. What the pillowcase contained were a few jumbled snapshots; an old, battered address book; some jewelry—silver bangles and a few pairs of gold earrings—whatever hadn't been pawned; various medicines, though she'd flushed the last of the hospital pills down the toilet before leaving; and all the money they had in the world, withdrawn from the bank the day before, as well as some worthless old coins and two credit cards. *If there isn't a cure, then there's no need to save for old age.* Gillian's mother must have told herself that. "We have to conserve our resources," she told Gillian. "Our treasure has to last until I'm better." That was the reason they found the cheapest motel they could to sleep in.

If you've seen one, you've seen them all: flat roofs; stuccoed cement on the outside; peeling tan or some-

[41]

times pink paint; cracked windowpanes, one or two boarded over; trash set off to one side. The entrance is through a broken screen door, into a half-lit room that contains a desk; a dull-faced clerk; a registration book; signs, nowadays, in Spanish and English, warning against unsafe sex and shared needles; and a vending machine. Behind the desk are a high stool and a telephone, the only one in the building. A guest who wants to make a call has to go back outside, walk twenty steps or so to the highway, and put money into the public phone that mostly truckers stop to use.

As depressing as the lobby is, the rooms are worse. They are uncarpeted, unair-conditioned and airless, smelling of mildew and damp. Exposed pipes run along the ceilings. Each room contains a narrow bed with the thinnest of mattresses, dingy linen, and a woolen blanket, usually gray, with ragged edges and holes. There is a sink in one corner that probably drips, perhaps with a mirror above it, sometimes chipped, sometimes missing. Above this place on the wall is a naked forty-watt light bulb screwed into a socket. There may be a second, similar light bulb suspended from a cord somewhere else in the room. There is also an old-model television set, not always working; a rod on one wall for hanging clothes; and a chain lock on the door.

The toilet, incredibly dirty and often out of order, is in a room at the end of the hallway. So is the shower, really just a faucet in the wall, a floor drain, and a plastic curtain, moldy at the bottom, with a drawstring at the top. Guests are given one thin white, stained towel each but are expected to bring their own soap. Those who don't can buy flakes in small envelopes from the lobby vending machine, which also dispenses stale candy and condoms. The towels, like sheets, aren't changed daily, and rooms get cleaned only between guests, just barely.

It was to a motel like this one that Gillian came with her mother. It was in a room like this one that Gillian's mother left her, with instructions to be good and a bag of groceries bought at the convenience store on the highway: white bread, peanut butter, dry cereal, individual containers of juice, potato chips, a bar of soap—you can fill in the rest.

"I'm off to get cured. I'll be back as soon as I can. Anyone asks you, tell them you're here with your mom, and she's gone out looking for work." Gillian's mom took the pillowcase with her but left Gillian a short stack of five- and ten-dollar bills. "Buy what you need—more food, magazines, whatever you like."

THERE ARE TIMES when even imagination seems hardly sufficient. What did Gillian do all week in that room? What did she think? How did she feel? Did she spend the whole day watching television? Did the television work? Did she venture outside, explore on her own, walk up and down the highway? Did she start to telephone her grandmother, then hang up when she heard the phone ring, not wanting to seem disloyal to her mother? Or did she stay put all week in that room, afraid of attracting anyone's attention: the authorities, passing truckers, women driving by with children of their own, drug pushers, fruit pickers, the homeless and crazies? I hope, for her sake, that her mother, or Gillian herself, packed a book, something to read, and reread, all those long hours until she was sick of it.

Surely, that time of the year, it had to have rained. Did Gillian lie in the bed then, pull the blankets around her head, and listen to the thunder? Did she dress up in her mother's clothes, wrap herself in bright-colored cottons, experiment with hairdos and her mother's makeup? Did she stand on the bed to peer in the mirror? Did she hold conversations aloud with herself? Or just in her head? Did she picture her mother coming back cured, or not coming back, ever? How much of the time did she cry? Was she ever not afraid? Well, I know for a fact one thing she did. She wrote letters and mailed them.

Even shabby motels have stationery. She must have begged a good supply from the listless clerk in the lobby, dog-eared paper and crumpled envelopes with PALM TREE MOTEL printed at the top. Probably she bought her stamps, borrowed a pen and pencil from him, too. She kept her messages brief and up-beat: *We're in Florida. The weather is fine. Wish you were here. Love, Gillian.* She enclosed her name in a heart. Some of the letters were illustrated with rough pencil drawings, sketches, cartoons of a holiday spent by a beach; labeled stick figures, herself and her mom, fishing from a yacht, watching entertainment on a dock, or herself walking a tightrope, dancing for money thrown into a hat, sitting behind a desk checking in guests, her photograph on the front page of some newsmagazine. In all the pictures, she and her mom seem happy and healthy. I got a few. She sent more to her grandmother.

"What can I do?" her grandmother said. "I'm worried sick, but she's only my grandchild. She still has her mother."

HOW MUCH EASIER it is imagining her mother's first week in Florida. Healing houses are a dime a dozen, and all of them are more or less the same. Cool-looking women in white clothes, with soft voices, sign you in, take your money, your jewelry, eventually whatever you have that's of value. It's a sliding scale fee—as much as they can get their hands on. They tuck you into a bed under clean and starched white sheets. You're seen by a man they call doctor, though he has no medical degree. He takes your pulse, feels your forehead, raises your lids to peer into your eyes, taps your feet. He prescribes, first, three days of fasting, during which you are to drink as much water and watered fruitade as you can.

"This is to flush out your system, help it rid itself of all its poisons. We are here only to help you cure yourself. You must learn to listen to your body."

Every day you will have a cocoa butter massage. Soft music is played to calm your mind. There are hot herbal baths. On the fourth day, you will begin eating soft foods: rice cereal, mashed chick-peas, flavored gelatin, rhubarb pudding. On the fifth day, you will be given a diet to continue at home. The doctor will see you for the second and final time. It's true you aren't cured yet, but, he explains to you, everything possible has now been done. The rest is up to you, he says. You must follow what your body tells you and, above all, have faith. He encourages you to refer your friends to his clinic; make sure they call ahead for reservations and to make financial arrangements. Then you are back on the street on your own, in Gillian's mother's case taking a taxi to the motel, where one look at her told Gillian her mother's condition was worse than before, plus her pillowcase was nearly empty.

Later that day, or perhaps the next, they went to the motel office to pay ahead on their bill. Gillian's mother's credit card was refused. It had been used up to its limit.

"Do you have another card?" the clerk asked, his tone flat, his eyes bored. But the second card was also refused. The clerk wasn't surprised. It happened a lot.

"Well, we were planning to move on anyway," Gillian's mother told him, turning away. They walked to the highway telephone, chilled by the unexpected change in weather, a Florida cold snap. They called Gillian's grandmother collect. She promised to wire money and send down their coats on the bus. They spent the night in the bus depot, huddled together, trying to get warm.

"We're waiting for a package," Gillian's mom told the woman at the ticket counter, who didn't care why they were there, would have let them stay regardless, was not about to put a mother and a child out on the street on such a cold night. Who would have imagined temperatures could drop so low in Florida in fall, or have imagined, even now Gillian's mom would be planning to stay?

6

Serpent's Milk and Whiskey

IN INDIA, they tell a story about a woman with no relatives of her own, only her husband and his family, his two parents and six married brothers, all of whom lived together. "The one who has no one at her father's place," they called her. They looked down on her for being an orphan and for never having had a dowry. When the rest of the family ate, she had to wait and collect the scraps they left in the pots, and eat them. Afterward, she had to wash the pots.

Things went on this way for some time. Then, when it was the season for offering food to dead ancestors, the relatives prepared sweet *khir*, rice pudding made with buffaloes' milk. Pregnant now, this woman craved the pudding, but she got only the half-burned crusts at the bottom of the pot. She didn't complain.

She wrapped them in cloth for her lunch, took the bundle with her when she went to fetch water, laid it down by the side of the well while she bathed.

A female serpent, pregnant too, smelled the *khir*, came out of her hole, and ate it. Then she went back to her hole. When the woman returned and found her food gone, she did not do as the serpent expected, put a curse on the thief whoever it was. No, she didn't. Instead, she said, "Poor woman who ate my lunch. She must be hungrier even than I. May God bless her." Of course, she had no clue as to who the real thief was. Nevertheless, the serpent was overjoyed hearing the blessing. You can imagine how seldom it is a serpent gets blessed.

"My family will be your family from now on," the serpent told the orphan, who was pleased to hear it and also astonished at such a turn of events. Not long after, the time came to prepare for the woman's first pregnancy ceremony. But who was to celebrate it?

"This woman is an orphan," her mother-in-law said. "She has nobody."

The young woman said, "Mother-in-law, please give me an invitation for the ceremony. It is for a distant relative." How happy she was to have an honorary family now to invite, even though they were serpents.

But, "Look everybody!" the mother-in-law said. "Our brotherless, sisterless, fatherless, motherless lady is out of her head. She has suddenly found a relative."

I think of this story when I think about Gillian going with her mother to visit her grandfather on the west coast of Florida—her mother's father, her grandmother's husband. He was no one Gillian knew. Her grandmother seldom spoke of him, and her mother did not speak of him at all. How was it then they could find him? Well, even missing people leave clues. There are driver's licenses, tax office records, utility bills, police logs, employment books; a person almost can't exist in this country without a social security number. There are, besides, intricate grapevines, lines of private information kept up among relatives and friends. I'd say, once she decided, it probably wasn't that hard for Gillian's mother to track down her own father.

"I'm broke, but I guess if you can get yourself here, you can stay," he told her on the telephone.

"That's that," she told Gillian gaily, hanging up. "Your grandfather says we should come." She bought two bus tickets with money Gillian's grandmother had wired.

So many stories have happy endings. In India, for instance, the orphan's serpent relatives all came to her pregnancy ceremony, dressed in festive robes, disguised as nobility. They brought with them lovely gifts, gold and silver and silk.

The orphan's in-laws were amazed. "Where did all these relatives come from?" they asked one another. "And so rich!" Right away they began preparing special foods to serve them. But the serpent mother called the orphan aside and said, "Tell your in-laws not to cook. We serpents can't eat ordinary food. Just have them boil milk and spice it." So that's what the orphan did. She explained to her mother-in-law that her relatives belonged to a caste that drank only spiced milk. "That is their prescribed food," she said.

When it was time for her serpent relatives to leave and go home, the orphan woman accompanied them, planning to return to her in-laws after her baby was born. When they arrived at the serpents' home, her honorary relatives turned back into snakes and took the young woman with them into their hole. The underground home was very beautiful, and the orphan was lovingly treated. Even so, she eventually grew tired of foods always made from milk, and she also missed the sunshine. After the birth of her son, she was ready to return to her husband's family.

Before she left, however, they shared a last meal of spiced milk. Then the grandfather serpent said to the girl, "Don't be afraid. Do as I say. I won't bite you. I want to give you a going-away present." He instructed her to put her hands into his mouth, first one and then the other, all the way down into his throat. She did so, and when she withdrew each arm, it was covered with gold bracelets, some of them emerald- and ruby-encrusted, and other valuable jewels. So that's the way she went home, with a fine baby boy and very wealthy. Why wouldn't she live happily ever after?

TOO BAD Gillian's grandfather's prescribed drink wasn't milk. It was whiskey, but it had not always been. I knew that man from way back when, almost to the day he stepped off the plane in New York, coming from St. Lucia. For sure, he was sober.

He was still just a boy then. He completed high school in Brooklyn, living with an aunt and an uncle. He studied hard, did well, worked his way through City College busing tables and washing dishes at night. He graduated magna cum laude with a degree in English literature. What for? Well, at least he could teach. Isn't that what people say? *Some* people say it. *If you can't do, then at least you can teach.*

"See, it's your accent," they told him. "Come back in a few years when you're speaking American." Had he majored in engineering, it would have turned out the same. It was nothing to do with his accent. What they truly didn't like was his dark honey-color skin, so even all over, and also the texture of his hair. In the end, he took the only job he was offered that didn't involve a broom. He became a liquor salesman for a wholesale distributor. It was already the 1950s.

He still believed in the American dream: an honest, reliable, hard-working man with education could get ahead. He worked hard and took business courses at night. Along the way, he fell in love and got married. Gillian's mom came along. He watched as others, whitemen without college degrees, younger than he and hired behind him, got promoted, were pushed ahead. Now and then, he tried drowning his sadness in drink. A family man, however, needs every penny he can put his hands on. He took on extra jobs: mail sorter on weekends, watchman, night clerk at a motel. The scarcity of his choices, he took to heart. As years went by, it turned his heart bitter. He began drinking more.

By the time Gillian's mom was in junior high school, her father was definitely an alcoholic, although outside the house he did a good job of hiding it. By the time Gillian's mom was ready for college, he'd quit selling liquor at all and only drank it. He left the company with the same business card he'd had when he started: JAMES WILLIAMS, AREA REPRESENTATIVE. He also left home, made his way south. In Florida, a man can fish for his dinner, doesn't need much in the way of clothing. He kept on drinking. Sometimes, he sold life insurance to cover his rent. It wasn't a lot.

The place he stayed was tumbledown, poorly kept, lacking amenities; but to Gillian and her mom it was more than satisfactory, compared with their recent motel on the highway.

"How am I gonna take care of you when I can't take care of myself?" Gillian's grandfather asked his only child. He stared hard at Gillian. "You sure got yourself a beautiful daughter." Gillian stared back, saw a half-bald, trembly old man in need of a shave, thin, with a potbelly, dribbles on his clothes, and a sour whiskey smell about him.

"Granddaughter," she said stubbornly, inside herself. But she knew it was nothing she could count on.

"You look after your mother now, hear," her grandfather told her. What I don't know is this: what else did he tell her? A man under the influence of alcohol will say anything, even to a child. Even his own child. Didn't he tell Gillian's mom, for instance, when she wasn't much older than Gillian, "You ruined my life. See, it's all your fault I am where I am. I was headed for bigger things, nearly had my business degree, would have made vice president in charge of marketing by now. Your coming along was an accident, forced my hand, made me marry your mother too soon. A family man, I had to give up my plans, become what I am, a whiskey salesman without any future."

Did he tell Gillian that, too? "Your mother ruined

my life." Was that why they left before they'd ever unpacked? Unpacked what? Their pillowcase? Their one valise containing soiled clothes and strips of colored cotton? Or did they leave because they saw no way to stay: no room, no bed, no food in the kitchen, no money to buy any, just a careless array of bottles of whiskey?

"Please, let's go home." Gillian must have said that even as she and her mother took to the streets.

"Can't go home," her mother must have told her, not willing yet to admit her condition. She wasn't willing to go home to die. She was still determined to live. But how? Without money, no home, hardly more than the clothes they were wearing.

So, look around! See those other people? How do they manage? I'd say it's pretty much the same no matter who you are. One night you find yourself on the street, no place to go. At first you're amazed; then you're bewildered. You can't believe what's happening is happening to you. Then, day by day, night by night, you learn what to do—take sink baths in filthy filling-station rest rooms, wash your hair there, ask passersby for change, eat scraps of food, rummage in garbage cans, take handouts from strangers. Finally, you're not even shocked when a well-dressed person offers you a doggie bag, leftovers scraped from her plate in a hotel restaurant.

By the time November came, Gillian and her mom

were regular street people. Thanksgiving Day morning found them standing in line outside a church, waiting patiently for hot turkey dinners.

"The year you turned two, your daddy gave away whole turkeys free to poor people on Thanksgiving Day. The turkeys came from where he worked. It was part of his job," Gillian's mother told her. "Now we're poor people ourselves. Who says good deeds go unrewarded?" Her tone was just as bitter as the weather.

Less than a month later, on a dreary, overcast day before Christmas, Gillian decided one more night on the streets, one more rainy night, would be more than she could bear. Her mother was too weak to protest. Gillian telephoned her grandmother collect.

"Please, wire us bus fare. We want to come home."

I CAN JUST see them standing there at the airport, in line to buy tickets. Gillian's grandmother was so relieved to hear from them she wired that much money. Now she can hardly wait to have them back, safe at home. But look how thin they both are. Gillian's mother is clearly very sick. Gillian has lost her little-girl look. I wonder they can appear as clean as they do, having been so long on the streets, and wonder, too, how they still maintain such an air of elegance. Even as Gillian's mother leans against the counter for support, it's not impossible to imagine her a dethroned queen from some faraway principality, down on her luck temporarily. I don't need to imagine the rest. I've heard it enough times, in detail.

Standing as close as she was, Gillian's mother overheard a conversation going on between the ticket agent and her customer. The customer was arranging for a discount, a half-price ticket, on account of someone's disability.

"I'm disabled, too," Gillian's mom informed the ticket agent when it was her turn. "Can I fly at a discount?"

"Yes?" said the ticket agent. "What's wrong with you?"

Gillian's mom leaned even closer. She spoke in a loud whisper.

"I have AIDS," she said. The agent's eyes opened wide. She took a step backward.

"Oh, I'm so sorry," she said. "Wait right here. I'll be back in a minute." But a man came instead. Gillian's mom flew half price, in an aisle seat. Gillian sat by the window, looking out. The only vacant seat on the plane was the one between them, with the pillowcase on it. The valise was under the seat in front.

When they arrived at La Guardia airport, Gillian's grandmother was there to meet them. "Oh, my God," she said. "What has happened to my child?" She could hardly believe what she saw. At home in her apartment, she ran hot baths for them. While they took turns soaking, she heated black bean soup and fixed a pan of corn bread. Then she fed them both and tucked Gillian's mother into her bed.

"Gillian can sleep with me on the sofa," she said. "We'll talk in the morning."

But when Gillian awoke the next day, her grandmother wasn't there. She'd left a pot of hot coffee, cold cereal, and a note on the table: *Help yourself. Gone jogging. See you soon.* That's how Gillian found out her grandmother had taken up running while they were gone.

"I'm in training. It runs in our family," she told them when she returned, and explained how some distant cousin or other from one of the Islands had once won an Olympic gold medal for track a long time ago. Even so, it was truly amazing, a woman her age taking up such a strenuous sport when she'd never been athletic before, unless you count dancing. "See, when you're running, there isn't room for anything else in your head. You forget all your problems."

Well, sure, that's fine while you are. But what happens when you stop? I worried about her. I worried she was headed for a breakdown. I worried about Gillian, too. With her mother too sick to take care of her, and her grandmother training as hard as she could, who would look after her, see to it she was properly fed, got caught up in school? What would become of her? What happened next was nothing I'd even considered.

7

Temporary Shelter

"GILLIAN'S WHERE?" I asked when her grandmother told me, thinking I'd probably misunderstood. She repeated the news.

"Oak Ridge, Tennessee."

I was certainly surprised to hear it, but nowhere near as surprised, I'm sure, as Gillian. Try hard enough, and I can almost hear exactly what her grandmother told her.

"It's only temporary. Uncle Henry's your father's brother; you're his own flesh and blood. He wants you to come, and so does Aunt Corinne. I've thought about it and thought about it—it's for the best, believe me. You see for yourself, your mother's in no condition to look after you properly. Most of the time, she's not even in her right head. What she did before, she can do again: drag you off to some Godforsaken place to camp out on the street like some homeless person. Do you want that to happen? So long as you're here, there's nothing I can do to prevent it.

"Besides, you'll like Tennessee. It's the country. There are mountains and rivers and trees. It's not like New York, drugs on every street corner, crackheads shooting at each other in broad daylight, children caught in crossfire. It won't be forever—just until your mother starts feeling better. We're trying to do what's best for you. You have a cousin there; you'll be with family. Smile, it's not the end of the world."

Maybe, maybe not; but having once pursued a story there, I can understand a person thinking that it might be. Oak Ridge is a city built on a site picked by the federal government in 1942 because of its isolation. It was built for one secret purpose and encircled by barbed wire fences to keep almost everyone from finding out. Federal, as it was, it remained entirely segregated so as not to offend whiteworkers from the South, including scientists. Though the army planned to avoid a military camp model, in fact that's what the old part of the city most resembles, even today.

Today, the city is best known for, and publicly boasts of, what was once its most secret secret. Oak Ridge was the site of the Manhattan Project; here, in what once was among the most beautiful and uncontaminated places in the country, the United States of America engaged in a crash project to produce uranium-235, the basic material that successfully fueled the first atomic bomb. The barbed wire fences have long since been torn down; the schools are no longer segregated; still many of those who work in this city wear badges, require security clearances. Who knows for sure what they do? And the contamination remains. There are NO FISHING signs in the creeks, warnings necessitated by accidentally dumped mercury, but no public warnings of nuclear waste, which some say is embedded in soil and in lakes, carried home on the bottoms of shoes before people knew its true danger. Those who work here, whose jobs depend on the government, claim it isn't so, insist there's no need to worry. Gillian's uncle Henry is one of them, an engineer at Oak Ridge National Laboratory.

"SURE, SEND HER HERE. We have plenty of room, and fresh air. You don't have to be concerned about drugs. This is a good place for children." Well, he worked in Oak Ridge, but he was also talking about where he lived, his one-family ranch house north of the city. It was a different school district, yet otherwise so intimately tied to the town to its south that most residents, when asked by outsiders where they were from, simply answered Oak Ridge.

"We're looking forward to having you join our family," Aunt Corinne told Gillian on the telephone.

"Your cousin DeeDee has already been spreading the word, telling everyone she knows she's getting an older sister."

"Cousin," Gillian said inside her head, and tried to picture this stilted-sounding aunt whom she'd never met. She barely remembered her uncle. She and her mom had visited him in Tennessee the summer after her father died, the year before her uncle got married. She thought they'd all gone to a zoo. Every Christmas since, he'd sent her a present—a toy, a book, something to wear—and once or twice a year he telephoned. Somewhere, her mother had a photograph of him, a round-faced, pleasant-looking, chubby whiteman with reddish hair and a good-natured smile that disclosed crooked teeth. In this way, he was not a total stranger. The only thing Gillian knew about DeeDee was her age, five years old last August. Now Gillian was about to meet her.

THERE ARE ONLY two reasonable ways to get to Oak Ridge, by car or by plane. Buses and trains do not stop there. Gillian flew. A flight attendant helped her change planes in Raleigh, North Carolina. Everything Gillian had on was new: a plaid jumper, white blouse, white lace slip and underclothes, black tights, and loafers. Even before the sun was up that morning, her grandmother had arranged her hair neatly in two twisted balls on either side of her head. The night before, she'd helped Gillian pack. Her belongings, including her pink Island stone from Aunt Sylvia, were in an old Samsonite suitcase that once was her father's, checked through by the airline. Gillian kept with her a small overnight bag her grandmother had bought especially for the trip. Into it her grandmother had put dried fruits and nuts, peanut butter and cheese crackers, a candy bar; also a few paperback books, hand wipes to use on the way, a toothbrush and toothpaste, a change of underwear, a pair of sneakers.

"You never know; airlines have been known to misplace a person's luggage," her grandmother told her, though this time they won't. "Whatever else you need, I can send."

Gillian had a window seat all the way, and gazed out. "Don't ask me anything about that trip," she'll say later. "I was too sad and angry to notice." When pressed, however, she does remember some few things about that day—landing, for instance.

"ALL THREE OF THEM were there to meet me. How much they looked alike was almost comical, each with reddish hair and very pale-complexioned. They stood so stiffly, side by side, you'd think they'd just stepped off some folk art calendar. Uncle Henry and Aunt Corinne are about the same height, but on him it looked short, and on her it looked tall. Something about her seemed out of proportion. Her shoes didn't help. They were flat, black cloth, and looked like an old person's bedroom slippers. 'They're from China. There's nothing like them for walking,' she announced to me on the way to the car. Even so, she managed to trip a few times.

"The ride to their house took over an hour. There wasn't a lot of conversation. DeeDee and I sat in back. We started out each of us leaning against an opposite door. Almost right away DeeDee began inching closer. I worried she'd end up in my lap, but no. She settled by my side, joined hands with me, and intertwined our fingers. 'I'm five. I go to kindergarten. Green is my favorite color. Pizza's my favorite food,' she said all in one breath. I'm certain I stared. I know she stared back, though how she could see through her hair, I don't know. Thick red curls fell over her forehead and into her eyes. I had to look twice to be sure they were blue. They're that dark in color. She has features like a dollbaby: pointy chin, puckered lips, buttony nose. What I noticed most about her was how sturdy she seemed, and also very determined. 'Are your seat belts fastened, girls?' her mother asked from the front. 'Mine is,' DeeDee said without moving, then snapped the middle belt around herself.

" 'I'm sure Gillian would like to wash up,' Aunt Corinne said the minute we arrived. 'The second room on the right is yours. There's an empty closet and chest of drawers. Uncle Henry's building you a bookcase.

Anything you need, let me know. You'll be sharing the bathroom at the end of the hallway with DeeDee. Towels are in the linen closet. Help yourself. We're very glad to have you here. Please feel at home.' It sounded weird the way she said it, as though we were in a movie, and she was saying lines from her part as hostess. 'I hope you like fish,' she added. 'It's what we're having for dinner.' While she cooked, Uncle Henry gave me a tour of the house. DeeDee came along, attached to my side like a Siamese twin.

"I suppose, as houses go, theirs isn't *that* large, but I was used to cozy apartments. Just the idea of a finished basement was new. That's where Uncle Henry had his workshop. There were windows all around the house, some at ground level, some below, and none of them had bars, or locks. Anyone could break in. The main floor was level with the lawn. What was to keep wild animals—rats, raccoons, snakes, poisonous spiders, for all I knew—from chewing their way in through the walls or creeping up from the finished basement through the floorboards? I looked down at DeeDee and decided not to mention it. No point, I thought, scaring a five-year-old. Besides, she was looking up at me so trustingly. She put one hand in mine. 'I'm glad you came, Gillian. I love you,' she whispered. 'Thank you,' I told her. What else could I say? I was glad to hear dinner was ready.

"Not that I wanted to eat; and even if I had,

everything was undercooked. The rolls were squishy. I looked around the table. It was hard to believe these three people were my relatives. Well, I told myself, it's just my father's family. I planned to stay not a single day longer than necessary. I was positive, now that my mom was home again, being looked after by Grandma, she'd start feeling better right away and insist I come back. That's when Aunt Corinne spoke up.

" 'I talked with the guidance counselor at your school,' she said. 'I think you'll be glad to know they plan to put you where you belong, in sixth grade. Whatever you missed this past fall, they'll let you make up in summer school.' Right that second, I felt my heart turn over. I had been counting all along on being back in New York by Easter.

" 'Can I be excused?' I asked.

" 'Me, too?' said DeeDee. She followed me to my room and sat on the floor.

" 'Want to hear a story?' I asked her. She nodded. I'd heard it from an old guy in a soup kitchen in Florida. He'd told it to me just to pass the time, the same reason I told it to DeeDee. Possibly, having fish for dinner had reminded me. This was the story.

" 'Ages ago, a girl caught a fish. It was a carp. She kept it for a pet and trained it. She taught it to live out of water; at first only for a few seconds, then a few minutes, then for hours at a time, and, finally,

forever. The two of them went almost everyplace together. Well . . .' I paused, the same as the guy in
Florida. Then I went on. 'To make a long story short,
one day, while the girl was taking her bath and the
fish was keeping her company, it fell into the bathtub
and drowned. That's it,' I said.

"But after DeeDee was gone from my room and I
was in bed, I told the story again to myself, only this
time I added a proper conclusion. 'So that's how that
was,' I said. 'Don't you be that way, Gillian. You see
where it can lead. A person who forgets where she's
from will always come to a bad end.' I knew Grandma
would never let that happen. 'She's sure to send for
me soon,' I told myself."

8
Letters

THAT FIRST January Gillian spent in Tennessee I sent her some books, along with a note.

Dear Gillian,
Your mother gave me your address. She said you like getting mail. I hope these amuse you.
Love, Isabelle Ramos

Gillian wrote back to thank me. Afterward, we corresponded often. I saved her letters. Gillian's dates were approximate. Her salutation was always the same: Dear Ms. Ramos . . .

& & &&

        February

———————,

  Thank you for the books. I already started
reading one. I like it so far. There's not much else
to do here. To get anyplace, you need a car, even
just to buy a Coke. There is no public
transportation and hardly any sidewalks. The
people here don't seem to mind.
  I don't care. As soon as Mommie starts to get
better, I'm going home. In the meantime, Mommie
said you'd love to hear from me. She said our lives
could be a book, and since you're a writer, you
could use them. If you ever do, please keep this in
mind. Coming to Tennessee was NOT my idea.
Well, I will write again soon.

          Your friend,
          Gillian

ॐ   ॐ   ॐ

February

——————— ,

February was definitely not the best time of year
for me to start school here. It is Black History
Month. Any other time, I might have gone
unnoticed. As it is, I'm asked a lot, "What are
you?" Can you believe such rudeness? "I'm part
Gypsy," I finally said. "From the West Indies." I
would have said New Yorker, but it sounded too
ordinary.

Do you remember Fiona, my friend who lived
with her mom in 2A? I wish both of them were
here now. I could definitely use my fortune told. I
wonder what happened to them after they moved
away. There are no Gypsies here, nor anyone from
the Islands either, so far as I can tell. Except for a
few children who look Asian, almost everyone in
my school is plainwhite. "Are you really a Gypsy?"
some of them asked. They wanted me to read their
palms, which I did to the best of my ability.

Your friend,
Gillian

ﻬ   ﻬ   ﻬ

February

——————— ,

Did I tell you my aunt Corinne works part-time
in a library? She says I should call her that, and I
do, for lack of any better name. I agree Corinne
would be rude, and Ms. Hardwick sounds too
formal. I'm sure she means well, but we are not
blood-related, and, not counting DeeDee and my
uncle, I think we have nothing in common. One
good thing about her job is that she brings books
home for me for school reports. One bad thing is,
then she wants to discuss them. I found this out
from one of them. It may help you see the kind of
place where my grandmother sent me to live. If you
are not interested, you can just skip the rest of this
letter.

Oak Ridge was built by the United States
government for its atomic bomb project. Even
though over 1500 blackworkers were hired—only
as dishwashers, janitors, furnace stokers, and so
on—no housing was built for them. Instead,
something called hutments were put up for them to
live in. But husbands and wives could not live
together, and children weren't allowed, period.

Each hutment was 16 by 16 feet square, for four to six residents. There was a stove in the middle of the floor for heat. In summer, the stove was taken out and one more person put in. Beds and a few folding chairs were the only furniture. The hutments had no closets or glass in the windows. There was no electricity and no running water. There was one central bathhouse with showers and toilets for every 24 to 36 hutments. After Florida, I can imagine how that was. The houses for whiteworkers had modern kitchens, indoor plumbing, and extra bedrooms for the children. If any blackperson ever complained, no matter how respectfully, he was secretly investigated and wound up having a permanent confidential government file.

I found this out from another book: in 1956, a local high school was integrated by court order. This meant twelve blackstudents started going there instead of being bused to Knoxville, fifteen miles away. Whitepeople stood outside the school every day, shrieking insults at them and threatening violence. The threats came true. Two years later, on a Sunday morning, the school was blown up. This happened in almost the same town where I'm living.

Well, I found out a lot more, but I don't want to bore you.

Your friend,
Gillian

❧ ❧ ❧

February

____________,

My report is finally done. Would you believe, after doing all that research I decided just to write a paper on Martin Luther King, Jr. But my teacher said no. Too many other students had already picked him. So then I took my uncle Henry's advice and interviewed Mr. Dixon, a very old AfricanAmerican man who actually once lived in a hutment. Now he owns an auto body shop. It's the only black-owned business in town. Uncle Henry knows him from the time Uncle Henry's van ran into a deer years ago. It was in the middle of the night.

During Mr. Dixon's hutment years, his job was mostly pouring cement. "I sure needed work that time," he said. He left his wife and children back home in Maryville. "Oak Ridge was no place for a man to bring his family, not for a blackman; but I needed the money. I try not to live in the past, but I'll tell you this—the way they did us blackfolks then, I wouldn't do that to anyone."

Your friend,
Gillian

ᚕ   ᚕ   ᚕ

March

——————— ,

    I talked to Grandma and Mommie both last night. Mommie was almost asleep. Grandma said she thinks about me all the time but doesn't call more so as not to interfere with my settling down. "Your job is to get adjusted," she told me. I can't imagine what she thinks I'm adjusting to, or why I'd ever want to settle down here in the middle of nowhere with people I hardly know. She said she'd spoken to you, and you were glad to get my letters. I'm glad to get yours, too. Except for three postcards from my mother, they're my only mail.

Take care,
Gillian

ð   ð   ð

March

—————————— ,

DeeDee, Uncle H, and Aunt C are in church this minute, Unitarian church. They asked me if I wanted to go. I said no. "We could go to a different church with you if you'd like," Aunt Corinne offered. I think she meant the Baptist church in Scarboro, which is black. We rode by it one day last week, and she pointed it out. I told them I'd rather stay home. I did not say what I thought, which was, why would I want to do that? In the first place, we are not Baptist, and in the second place, I have a bone to pick with God right now for the situation I'm in. I know no one wants to hear about it, including Mommie and Grandma. I'm only telling you to get it off my chest.

Sincerely,
Gillian

P.S. I got a B+ on my Black History report. I think I would have gotten higher, but I lost points on account of not typing.

࿙   ࿙   ࿙

March

—————————,

Today Aunt Corinne took DeeDee and me for
new sneakers. Afterward, we went to Time Out
Deli. I thought I'd gone to heaven. Finally, normal
food on bread that wasn't gluey. I ordered a veggie
sub with melted cheese, and fried onion rings on
the side—plus extra pickles. DeeDee ordered the
same, then made a face when it came. "It's very
tasty," she said, chewing.

She also insisted on sneakers exactly like mine.
Of course, they didn't have a pair in her size. So I
switched. Now we both have low-cut white ones
with little balls at the ends of the laces. It was a
small sacrifice for me to make. Who cares what I
wear here? I think in Tennessee even Mommie
would forget about fashion. In this house, the
fashion is to keep covered up at all times. I have
never seen such modest people in my life. Even
DeeDee always wears a robe over her nightgown.

"Please, Gillian, I'm using the bathroom," she
told me when I first came, and locked the door.
"But you're just a baby. You don't even have

anything to hide," I said. "Going to the bathroom is private," she answered.

When I think about my bubble baths with Mommie, I could cry. I tell myself soon I'll be back in New York. Last time Mommie called, she sounded much better. Well, I do know about AIDS, but Grandma says we have to have faith, and I'm trying.

Write soon,
Gillian

❧   ❧   ❧

April

—————————,

Thank you for the bagels. I put them in the freezer right away. Every day I heat one up for breakfast. They are delicious. DeeDee put a garlic one in the microwave. I warned her it would come out like rubber, and it did. She ate it anyway. "I like it, Gillian," she said. I think everything she's ever tasted has first been microwaved. "Just wait until my mom comes this summer and cooks

callaloo soup," I told her. That's my big news.
Mommie promised she'd visit in August.

Love,
Gillian

 è   è   è

April

——————— ,

   I am glad I have you to write to. I can tell you
things and know you won't tell Mommie. If she
knew, she'd only feel worse, and she feels bad
enough now. I try to keep a positive attitude, but
some days are so depressing. Yesterday, for
instance. I had to read an autobiography for school.
I picked one by a ChineseAmerican artist, Dong
Kingman. When he was DeeDee's age, he already
knew what he wanted to be. He saw a book in a
store window with a picture on the cover of a
yellow tiger. He wanted to learn how to draw it.
He begged his father to buy him the book so he
could practice, but his father said no. It cost too
much money. A few days later, Dong stole some
money, bought the book, and practiced drawing the
tiger until he got it right. His father found out
about the money and beat him. His father also

framed the picture and hung it in his store. "My son drew that tiger," he told all his customers. Afterward, he took Dong with him wherever he went. I felt so sad when I read that. I know, no matter what I do now, or how well, no one will ever be as proud of me. Mommie is too sick, and Grandma is too busy looking after her and running.

Did I tell you, when Mommie comes here in August, Grandma is going to Italy to be in a marathon?

Take care,
Gillian

May

——————,

Thank you for your nice letter and the box of colored pencils. Please don't worry. I feel better already. May is such a pretty month here, it would be hard staying depressed. Wildflowers grow everywhere. I decided to try drawing some, but this is what happened.

I put on my boots because of poisonous snakes and walked to the highway. Although everyone here says you don't have to worry, I do. Anyway, it turned out I was worrying about the wrong thing. I didn't see any snakes. Instead, I saw a naked man. He wasn't totally naked. He had pulled his pants down, and not for the purpose of going to the bathroom. When he saw me, he waved his "thing" in my direction. Naturally, I took off running and didn't stop until I got home. Aunt Corinne called the police. Nothing came of it. However, I didn't get to draw any flowers, and I don't plan to go back and try either.

Your friend,
Gillian

🐌   🐌   🐌

May

——————,

Mother's Day has come and gone. I hope yours was happy. I sent Mommie a card. I sent Grandma one, too—plus money from my allowance to buy Mommie flowers. Mommie called from the hospital to say how much she liked them. She is just in for some tests. She was coughing a lot, but so far the X rays show her lungs are not damaged.

I know from listening that Mommie is on public assistance now. Grandma told Uncle Henry, and he discussed it with Aunt C. It was her only choice if she wanted her hospital bills paid.

Take care,
Gillian

↊   ↊   ↊

June

——————— ,

Last Sunday was Father's Day. DeeDee made Uncle H a plaster imprint of her hand, and also a card. She made me write on it TO A GREAT FATHER AND UNCLE, then sign it. I never signed a Father's Day card before. "Was my dad a lot like you?" I asked Uncle Henry. "Not really. Well, he was much younger," he said. If I ever find out any more about my father, I think it won't be from my uncle. He is not an easy person to talk to, believe me.

Love,
Gillian

&a.   &a.   &a.

July

——————,

Summer school has started. I'm taking math and typing. A girl from California named Julianne is in my class. This is her second time living in Tennessee. Her father is a scientist at the lab. She says her whole family could hardly wait to come back, even though it's just for two years. I didn't ask her why. Maybe they like seeing deer. I almost bumped into a baby one yesterday when I was getting off the school bus. It was crossing the road.

Love,
Gillian

&a.   &a.   &a.

July

——————,

Against my better judgment, and to keep Aunt Corinne happy, I finally invited Julianne to dinner. Imagine my surprise when wild mushrooms turned up on the table. Aunt Corinne collects them. It's her hobby. Who would have guessed? I mean, everything else she cooks comes from a can, and now this. "Aren't wild mushrooms poisonous?" I asked. I meant deadly. I once saw a movie in which wild mushrooms were the weapon of choice. "Some wild mushrooms are poisonous. You have to know the right ones to pick," Aunt C answered. "I have studied mushrooms for years. I never pick wrong."

That's all well and good, but she can only mean, so far. Julianne ate hers happily. It turned out she knew all about them from her father. He had researched them at work, looking for new medicines. "We got to eat the ones he didn't use," she told us. "At least, the ones that weren't poisonous. The main thing to know about mushrooms is never mix them with alcohol or eat too many." Naturally, I didn't eat any.

Take care,
Gillian

    🐸   🐸   🐸

July

—————,

I went with Aunt Corinne last week to the

Clinch River Raptor Center. It is in a public middle school in Clinton. I looked up the word. Raptor comes from the Latin, meaning "plunderer." Raptores is the order of wild birds that are predators—owls, hawks, and eagles, for instance. The ones at the center were all brought there, hurt, usually from being hit by cars, or caught in traps or shot, which is illegal. If they get better, they're released. If not, they're "put down," which means killed. They feed them mice, bought for that purpose. Most of the mice are dead. The leftover dead ones get frozen. Those not yet dead get put into the birdcages and are covered over with straw to keep them alive until the birds eat them.

Aunt C told me about a woman who wanted to volunteer. She'd read about the center in the paper. "It's a wonderful thing you are doing," she said on the phone. When she got there, she was horrified. "Couldn't you feed them something else?" she asked.

"We could," Aunt Corinne told her. "However, that's what they eat." I saw Aunt Corinne's point, but I understood how that other woman felt, too.

Love,
Gillian

P.S. Mommie is out of the hospital. "I'm feeling much better," she told me. She said all her systems were go, and her doctor could hardly believe how healthy she was for a person with AIDS. I can hardly wait to see her in August. I'm praying she'll take me home with her when she goes.

August

——————— ,

We went to see DeeDee in a play yesterday at her day camp. She stood up straight and said all her lines perfectly. When a little boy forgot his, DeeDee covered her mouth with one hand and whispered them to him. I think she stole the show, as they say. I was so proud of her. Summer school is over tomorrow, thank goodness.

I can't remember if I told you this before, but last week DeeDee took a snapshot of me to camp. "This is my cousin from New York, but she's really West Indian," she told the other campers. "She is not either. She can't be your cousin. She's not even white," they said. DeeDee insisted. It started a fight. That got the counselor's attention. The counselor sided with the other children.

The next day, Aunt Corinne went to camp with

DeeDee. When she came home, she was still angry. "Next time some child brings a picture of a relative to show, I think that counselor will know enough simply to say 'how nice,' " Aunt Corinne told Uncle Henry. I was surprised at first, but then I thought, well, sure—Aunt Corinne was only sticking up for DeeDee.

Mommie will be here next week. You may not hear from me for a while, as I probably won't have much time to write.

Love,
Gillian

August

———————,

Mommie's visit has come and gone. Grandma had to pay for her plane ticket, as public assistance doesn't cover things like that. Mommie looked much worse than I expected. I had to help her a lot: bathing, doing her hair, trying to get her to eat more. She felt up to doing only one sight-seeing thing, which was going to a quilt show in Knoxville. Afterward, we all ate lunch in an AfricanAmerican restaurant. Would you believe, I had corned beef on rye with pickles. It turned out the owners were from Brooklyn. Naturally, DeeDee had the same. Mommie had soup. "I love your mom. I hope she's better soon," DeeDee told me after we put Mommie on the plane. I hope so, too. Anyway, the plan now is for me to go home over Christmas, at least for a visit.

Love,
Gillian

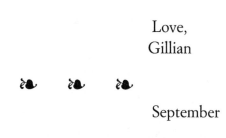

September

——————— ,

School has started. I'm in seventh grade, but it's still in the same middle school as last year. Most of my class is also the same, except for Julianne, who is in an accelerated program this year. I probably would be, too, if not for missing so much school last fall.

A lot of the girls in seventh grade wear bras now. Thank goodness I don't. I'm trying to eat less and exercise more, hoping in that way not to start periods either. I don't need them. I don't ever want to have children. They're too much worry and responsibility. Please don't mention anything about this to Mommie or Grandma. Did you know

Grandma placed third in her age group in Italy? I don't know how many others ran in it, though. I was too shocked by her latest news to ask—she has gone back to college to get a Ph.D. in sociology.

Love,
Gillian

&

&

&

October

———————,

When I came home from school yesterday, DeeDee was in my room, on her knees in my chair. She was wearing my bathrobe and peering into the mirror. "What are you doing?" I asked, trying to sound strict. I thought I shouldn't encourage her, but really, she looked so funny it was hard not to laugh. "I'm practicing," she said. "Practicing for what?" I asked. "Practicing to look like you," she told me, staring hard into the mirror. She was frowning, with her eyebrows pulled together and her head tilted that way I know I do. I almost fell onto the bed, giggling.

At that moment, she certainly did look like me. We have the same pointy chin, for one thing. But what I mean is, her expression was like mine.

"Why do you want to look like me?" I asked her. "Because I love you," she said. "And also because you're beautiful." Of course I had to hug her then. "I love you, too," I told her.

Love,
Gillian

❧   ❧   ❧

November

——————,

My birthday is over now, and so is Thanksgiving. Grandma called both days, but Mommie was asleep. I hope your Thanksgiving was better than mine. Everyone sat around all day waiting to eat. Dinner was very late because Aunt Corinne forgot to turn on the oven after she'd put in the turkey. Also, there were no sweet potatoes, the stuffing came from a box, and the gravy was canned. Still, I guess compared with last year I shouldn't complain. Except, last year Mommie was with me. I'm glad Christmas is coming and I can go home.

Love,
Gillian

ð   ð   ð

December

————————— ,

Only ten more days. I already have my plane
ticket, and all my presents are wrapped. I bought
Mommie a red and gold afghan. I told the woman
in the store how Mommie was always cold, and it
was just the right gift. The woman said she'd made
it herself but was putting it on sale for the holiday,
which was how come I could afford it. I made
DeeDee a rag doll in home ec, with orange yarn
hair and sewn-on blue eyes. It's stuffed with old
panty hose. I bought clothes for it in the drugstore.
I bought chocolates for everyone else. I don't have
any money left over for cards now. I hope you have
a Merry Christmas anyway, and a Happy New
Year.

Love,
Gillian

P.S. I'm also all packed. "You are coming back,
right?" DeeDee asked. I didn't have the heart to
say no, but I'm sure when Mommie sees how much
help I can be, she'll beg me to stay. "Please,

Gillian," she'll say. "I NEED you in New York." Of course I'll miss DeeDee, but it's not as if she can't ever come to visit.

December 19

Dear Ms. Ramos,

Thank you for your phone call. I'm sorry I couldn't talk more. I'm sure you understand. Uncle H is flying to New York with me tomorrow for the funeral. Maybe then I'll start to believe Mommie is dead. Right now, I know it's not possible.

Sincerely yours,
Gillian

9

Dearly Beloved

HARDWICK, Alonya Claire. Dearly beloved mother of Gillian Kameesha, devoted daughter of Verena Williams, on December 17. A memorial service will be held Wednesday, 11 A.M., at the Cathedral of St. John the Divine.

CLIMB THE STEPS slowly; peek in at the door. A funeral is going on. Well, there is no casket. Gillian's mom has already been buried. It was a very private ceremony, attended only by Gillian's grandmother. "Somebody had to be there, but it didn't take us both," she'd explained to Gillian. I think her true reason was this: she didn't want Gillian to hear that awful sound the first dirt makes falling on the coffin. It's a sound you don't ever forget. That's what the old people used to say. Now Gillian's grandmother and I are almost old people ourselves. I picture her as she must have stood that day, alone by the graveside, watching helplessly as her only child's body was laid to its rest. Now the thud of the dirt still resounds in her head, but she's finished her crying. What about Gillian, though, who never even got to tell her mother good-bye? Doesn't she also need time to cry? If you were to ask me, I'd say yes.

But sssh! Don't ask just yet. The organ is silent. The service has started. The reverend begins: "Dearly beloved, we are gathered here this morning not to mourn a death, but to celebrate a life." It is the message Gillian's grandmother instructed him to give. "I want you to remember your mother alive," she told Gillian. I look at Gillian, seated in the first row, second seat from the aisle to your right as you enter, her grandmother and her uncle on either side; and I wonder, does she?

She certainly looks composed. "I don't remember a single thing about that service," Gillian will say in years to come. "It's a total blank. Except I remember this. All day I had a pressing need to use the bathroom." It's true; she's gotten up several times already, squeezed past either her grandmother or her uncle, and gone out through the side door. But she's settled down now, dry-eyed, looking at the floor. Her uncle's left arm rests on the bench behind her head. Her grandmother's right hand touches Gillian's left knee. If Gillian is consoled by their closeness, she gives no sign. In fact, you could say she seems almost not present. Her body is here, but I think her spirit is somewhere else. I think she's already acting on her grandmother's advice—remembering her mother alive and still well. For all I can tell, her mind is on bathing. I imagine her imagining herself DeeDee's age and still happy. There's not even a glimmer of sadness ahead. She feels her own self sinking into a nice warm tub, her skin flushes slightly, and she hugs herself with her arms. She's surrounded by bubbles; inhaling, smells herbs; and her mother is right there behind her, soaping Gillian's back, untangling her long dark hair, humming melodies from hymns.

Gillian looks up. She has missed the homily. The choir is singing, and she hears her mother's voice, her heavenly soprano, rise in harmony, as on so many Sundays past; and then it fades away and is gone.

Do I imagine this, or do I actually see Gillian's body shiver, as though plucked from a sauna into sudden cold air, and nobody nearby with a towel to wrap her? I watch her put the tip of her right thumb into her mouth and suck hard, a childish practice she gave up years ago to please her mother. I'm struck by this thought—with her mother dead, Gillian's free to take up old habits. Who's going to stop her? Just then,

I hear the reverend intone, "Because Jesus was raised from the dead, we, too, shall be raised."

Gillian takes her thumb from her mouth, clasps her hands, moves her lips. I wonder if she's praying he's right, praying for life everlasting and this, above all—for the Holy Ghost. Because surely if there is One, there can be more. And if that is true, Gillian can pray for her mother to come back and be with her forever. The organist resumes playing. Gillian, and everyone, stands. Relatives file from the chapel, followed by friends of the family. They are directed to a room down the hall where coffee will be served, and refreshments.

But who are all these people, crowded together so intimately in this small room? Some are friends of Gillian's grandmother's from work, from school, from running; some are former friends of Gillian's mom's, fellow actors, singers with her in choir; not a single teacher from her old school is here. Neither is her father, who I'm sure was notified. Gigi-ma and Aunt Sylvia, of course, are present. So are some other relatives: distant cousins; two paternal, and elderly, uncles; and someone's ancient aunt who is visiting from Martinique. They all want to kiss Gillian's cheek, stroke her face, touch her hair. Gillian appears confused by so many strange, or forgotten, faces; overwhelmed by so much chatter. Clearly, she is relieved when this coffee hour is over and they can go home, she and her grandmother, three of her grandmother's oldest friends, and Uncle Henry, squeezed into the large black car rented for this occasion.

Once she is there, though, back in her grandmother's apartment, Gillian's despair finds no easement. New guests arrive, there is no abatement to the endless murmur, muted laughter, as old friends remember old times and share a tender good-bye. But for Gillian, there is no consolation. She feels sick to her stomach, and the pungent, spicy smells of food cooking do not help. She closets herself in the bathroom, bends over the toilet, choking, and tries to throw up. She can't. Her mouth fills with saliva, and Gillian spits it out into the bowl. Her grandmother finds her, coaxes her to the sofa, has her lie down, and tucks two blankets around her. Gillian lies there stiffly for hours, eyes closed, as though willing herself to shut out all sensations. Surely she believes if she can only stay this way long enough, everyone will go home; she will be alone with her grandmother and start feeling better. It's not much trouble surmising the rest.

Uncle Henry is the last guest to leave.

"You're welcome to stay. There's always room for one more," Gillian's grandmother says, wondering as she says it where she can reasonably put him.

"Thank you, but I've already reserved a hotel

room," Uncle Henry answers. "I figured you two would have plenty of catching up to do. I'll telephone in the morning."

"We've a busy day ahead of us," Gillian's grandmother says after he's gone. She outlines tomorrow's plans as Gillian undresses, gets ready for bed. A visit to the old apartment so Gillian can select what mementos she wants. Next, department store shopping for clothes to take back to Tennessee. "I'm sure you've about outgrown all your old ones," her grandmother says brightly.

"I'm sorry, what did you say?" Gillian asks. She feels somewhat the same way she did when she first heard her mother was dead—as though struck by sudden deafness; breathless, as if suffering from an unexpected blow to her stomach.

"Your mother died at half past ten," her grandmother had told her then on the telephone, just past midnight.

"I'm sorry. What did you say? I can't hear you," Gillian had answered. Her grandmother said it again. Gillian handed her uncle the phone, wordless.

"I'm so sorry," he said. Gillian heard the words fine, but outside any sensible register.

"Mommie is dead?" she finally said back. It was the best she could do, but she didn't believe it.

She's having trouble this minute believing her grandmother's current message. Nor does her grandmother's further explanation help. Plus this time she doesn't say one word about temporary. "See, you need a family. You have an uncle and aunt and a cousin in Tennessee. Here you have only me, and I'm always so busy. Between work and school and running around, I'm simply not home enough to look after you properly. Before Mommie died, we discussed it. She agreed with me. 'I want what's best for Gillian,' she said."

"Then she shouldn't have died," Gillian mutters under her breath, so low her grandmother has to strain to hear her, and even then she can't be sure she's heard right.

"Your mother loved you more than anything. Believe me, if she could have held on, she would have, if only to see you grow up. Be fair, Gillian. What we want isn't always possible." Gillian's grandmother stares straight into Gillian's eyes and speaks slowly for emphasis.

Gillian, however, is in no mood to be fair. She knows what she knows. She thinks back to Darlene, her sometime baby-sitter years ago. Darlene's mother came down with bone cancer when Darlene was still in grade school. "Don't worry," she used to tell Darlene. "I'm not going anyplace at least until I see you graduate from high school." And she didn't either. She went to Darlene's graduation ceremony in a reclining wheelchair, almost a stretcher. She was boneless and thin, with creased gray, parchmentlike skin; but her eyes shone with pride.

She died three weeks later, but first she'd lived for her child. She's the kind of mother I should have had, Gillian tells herself. I'd say, unfairly, because although the story is true as far as it goes, I, too, knew that family.

Darlene had a younger sister, Janelle. Janelle had just finished fifth grade the summer her mother died. Her mother never so much as saw Janelle graduate from junior high. Even a mother's love can take her only so far.

I'm thinking this minute of Gillian's grandmother. I watched, through those final weeks and days, as she took such good care of her only child, Gillian's mom. She did everything she could to make her more comfortable. She bathed her, fed her, combed her hair, changed her soiled linens and underwear.

"The most terrible part was, in the end, there was nothing I could really do for her," she said. Who can blame Gillian's grandmother for choosing to be alone now? If she believes hard work and study can cushion her grief, let her try. I'm not surprised she's running as fast as she can. Before she can be much help to Gillian, I think she will need to get hold of herself. Right this minute, though, she'd probably settle just for finding her eyeglass case.

"I don't understand it. Where can it be? I'm always so careful about putting it down." It isn't as if she were missing her glasses. Even so, she can't seem to stop looking. "I'm sure under normal circumstances it wouldn't seem such an insurmountable problem," she says, enlisting Gillian's help. But these are not normal circumstances, and for the next few days, Gillian and her grandmother will misplace a lot: the door key, the butter dish, Gillian's left shoe, the toothpaste tube, the telephone book. Searching gives them something to do, because of course it isn't really the key, or the eyeglass case, or the butter dish; not the shoe, or the toothpaste tube, or the telephone book. It's a daughter who's missing, a mother. What can a person expect who can't even keep track of her eyeglass case?

Gillian finds it in the morning on the kitchen counter, where they'd looked before. She's up early on account of a bad dream. In it some mother has died, leaving three children behind. "Three things you must do for me when I'm gone," she had warned them. But they hadn't. Maybe they couldn't remember, or didn't know how, or, like Gillian, had been struck by sudden deafness when faced by tragedy and never heard a word. In any event, they didn't do as their mother had asked, and now she can't rest in her grave. Instead, she stalks the earth and invades their dreams. If only they knew what three things to do, they'd do them and get some sleep at night. It was at this point in her dream that Gillian awakened.

"Was there something in particular Mommie wanted to tell me at the end, a final request, something she wanted me to do?" Gillian asks her grandmother at breakfast.

Her grandmother looks surprised, then thinks about the question. "You mother wanted you to be a good person and hoped you'd grow up happy." Watching Gillian push food around on her plate, her grandmother adds, "I'm sure she also wanted you to eat."

Obediently, Gillian picks up her cold roll and chews on it. She'll find hot food hard to face for a while. Just the smells of food cooking will make her feel ill, bring back that awful day of her mother's funeral when guests chattered, laughed, and ate as if her mother were alive and only in the next room, instead of somewhere underground, lying cold and dead. Except for not eating, though, Gillian behaves well, and I don't mean that day only, but for some time to come. It's her concentration that keeps breaking down.

She can barely bring herself to look around her old apartment when they get there. A photograph album, some loose snapshots, and a dark paisley shawl that belonged to her mother are all she picks out to take away with her. She's even more indifferent when it comes to shopping. "You decide," she tells her grandmother in the crowded department stores, ignoring all the holiday decorations. One outfit's as good as another—what does Gillian care what she wears in Tennessee?

There she is, now, on the airplane, in one of her new outfits, something blue with white trim. Her seat belt is fastened, her face is turned toward the window for takeoff. Uncle Henry is sitting beside her.

"Are you doing okay?" he asks.

Gillian nods. Uncle Henry closes his eyes, preparing to sleep, even though it's still morning. It's hard to believe a whole week has passed since they left Tennessee. Christmas is over, but they've hardly noticed. Gillian's stay in New York has gone by in a blur.

Later, she will say of this flight, the same as of her mother's service: "I really don't remember it. It's a total blank. My mind was numb."

10

Talking to the Walls

"SPRING IS COMING, and nothing can stop it now." That's according to some local boy. The hillsides are covered with redbuds and dogwood, all sorts of wildflowers; any minute now, bouquets of white Cherokee roses. It can be hard to resist. Especially for a city child, Gillian's aunt and uncle think. Therefore, they are pleased but not *that* surprised by the good adjustment Gillian seems to be making.

"I couldn't be more satisfied with her progress," Aunt Corinne tells Uncle Henry almost daily. "It's nothing short of a miracle how well she's settling down," she tells Gillian's grandmother on the telephone the last Sunday of every month.

Gillian's grandmother, of course, is glad to hear it, and also it confirms her belief. Her calling more often would only be disruptive. She's doing her best to settle down, too—working, studying, still running.

"Keeping busy's the main thing. Thinking can drive you crazy if you let it," she says to Gillian. But what's a person to do about sleeping and visitants who come by night, especially one's mother? Here's an example:

Gillian dreams of her mother alive underground, still breathing when they put her in her coffin, though just barely. It would have been hard to detect, even for a doctor. You could forget about finding a pulse. Now her mother is trying to push open the lid. Her painted fingernails are long, and strong, and bright red; but her arms, and her wrists, and her hands are wasted from her illness and powerless to push. Gillian awakes before she can help, her own fingernails digging into the palms of her hands, making impressions that will last until morning.

Here's another: Gillian dreams her mother has returned. Sometimes she's fully recovered. Other times she is still very stick, but hanging on. "Don't you worry, Gillian," she says those times. "I won't let go until there's a cure." She is looking forward to resuming her old life with Gillian, moving back into their apartment. Gillian doesn't know how to break the news, how to tell her mother she's dead, that the apartment's been given up, and that she, Gillian, is now living in Tennessee with her father's whitefamily.

When she awakes, she thinks—for sure, Mommie will understand. These are, after all, exceptional circumstances.

Finally, there's this dream. Gillian's whole family is in it; her grandmother and mother, Gigi-ma and Aunt Sylvia, even DeeDee and her parents are in it. But none of them are together. Each is somewhere else, and in imminent danger. This one is in a typhoon; that one is sick; someone is sound asleep, about to burn up in a fire. Sometimes they travel, hold tickets on planes that won't make it or trains that derail. Miraculously, no one dies. Gillian knows in her sleep, though, she is responsible for all of their safety. Only she can keep them alive. But it's too big a job. She cries out in her sleep, awakens herself. She's faced with the news all over again; her mother is dead.

Some nights she doesn't awaken herself. Some nights Aunt Corinne hears her first. Then she tiptoes quickly into Gillian's room, shakes her, and whispers, "Wake up, Gillian. You're having a bad dream." She says it the way people do, meaning it's just in your head; it can't harm you. But there are those who would say that's not true. They have science on their side. There are numerous well-documented cases of a mysterious phenomenon in which sleepers die from bad dreams. In the Philippines, it's called *bangungut*, the same word used for "nightmare." Japanese call it *pokkuri*. Young men of Asian ancestry, removed from their homes, seem especially prone to it. Circumstances are always similar.

A person goes to bed well, nothing the matter. In the middle of the night, he cries out in his sleep; not a loud cry, more like a whimper, soft and surprised. When those who hear rush to his side, they find him dead, his eyes wide open as if he'd seen something in his sleep or on awakening. Some say a ghost. Physicians who deliberate on the syndrome discuss other possibilities: cardiac abnormality, for instance; or vitamin deficiency. Regardless of theory, the result is the same—death comes to a sad young person far from home. Well, loneliness is one thing, but try to imagine a dream so powerful it stops the heart.

DEEDEE, safe at home and only six, has had some experience with bad dreams herself, though not lately. The first few weeks after Gillian's mother died, DeeDee began worrying about her own. Some nights, she awoke crying. Then her mother would come to see what was the matter. "Don't be silly. Nothing's going to happen to me," she'd tell DeeDee. "And even if something ever did, you'd still have Daddy," she always added. DeeDee wasn't entirely convinced.

"What if something happens to you *and* Daddy? If both of you die, who will take care of me?" DeeDee asked.

"Don't worry. Look at me," her mother answered.

"See how healthy I am." DeeDee stopped worrying. She's too young yet to know how fast a healthy person can get sick. But she does understand about nightmares. Also, since her bedroom is right next to Gillian's, DeeDee is most often the one who's awakened when Gillian calls. Each time, she gets up out of her own warm bed and hurries into Gillian's.

"Don't be afraid, Gillian. I'm here," she says then, wrapping her arms around Gillian's neck, patting Gillian's face with one chubby hand until both girls fall back asleep.

I think it's finding them wrapped together so tightly that way so many mornings that makes Gillian's aunt finally decide to seek help for Gillian. "Too much closeness can't be good for either one," she tells her husband. His response surprises her.

"Ahh, leave them," he says, but in a voice so gentle and with a look so far away, it makes her wonder. She peers at him closely, hoping to decipher what's in his mind. How can she? Even he can barely retrieve the past that lies there. The vision he sees is at most a blur: two young boys tangled together in one narrow bed, holding on to each other as if for dear life. Then it's gone like a dream in the morning. He can't explain what he hardly remembers. Nor does he object when his wife makes an appointment to speak to the school psychologist about Gillian. Though he doesn't mention it, he's worried, too. Even in this otherwise all-whitefamily, Gillian's pallor has become obvious to him, and also the dark rings beneath her eyes. Not that he believes a psychologist can help.

"She seems to be adjusting fine in the daytime," Aunt Corinne says at school. "Sometimes she has trouble sleeping at night." Fortunately, the psychologist has a plan. Gillian's aunt explains it at home.

"Of course, it's your decision," she says in that way she has that Gillian hates. "But it does seem a bit of good luck that a program like this is getting under way now." An after-school club for children with problems will meet with the school psychologist every Friday. The students will come from several schools. "It's to be called the Banana Splits because so many problems have to do with divided families. Just talking over what's on your mind often makes a person feel better," Aunt Corinne says.

Who knows? Maybe she's right. There are plenty of stories to back up her theory. I think of this one, for instance, about an overweight widow from Tamil who lived with her two sons and their wives. All four berated her from morning to night. There was no one to whom she could complain. Keeping all her sorrows in, she grew fatter and fatter. Now her children criticized her even more. One day, she wandered off by herself away from town. She came to a deserted shack that lacked a roof and had no windows. She went inside and felt sadder than ever. Then she spoke up, addressing first the wall in front of her. She told all her grievances against her older son. As she finished, the wall tumbled down under the weight of her woes. At the same time, the woman grew thinner. Next she turned to the second wall and told her grievances against her first daughter-in-law. As she finished, that wall fell, too, and the woman grew still thinner. And so it went with the third wall and her second son, and the final wall and that son's wife. Standing in the ruins, that woman felt lighter and happier than she had in a very long time. Then she went home.

But see, those walls didn't talk back. It wasn't like sitting in a classroom listening to true-life horror tales.

THERE ARE fifteen children in Gillian's club altogether: nine boys and six girls, in grades five through seven. I've changed their names for reasons of privacy. These are only some of their stories.

Samantha's problem has to do with money. Or possibly she finds finances easier to discuss than something more personal. Her real dad and her stepdad have both been laid off, and left town. "My stepdad can't stay with us anymore on account of we don't have a phone. If a job came along, no one could reach him," Samantha says sadly. "My mom's the only one in the family who still has a job, and it's only part-time. There aren't any benefits. 'Don't worry,' she tells me. 'Everything will be okay.' But I think she's lying.

Every day, it's as if I have a worry in my heart, and I can't stop thinking about it." Not having any money can be a lot of stress on a child, the other children decide.

Wayne thinks not having a real mom is worse. He's been in foster care for two years. Before that, he was adopted. "My mom gave me back when I was nine," he tells the class.

Whispering fills the room. "You can't give a child back, can you?" the other children ask one another.

"She just picked up the phone and called the agency," Wayne adds. "She explained to them things hadn't worked out. Too bad she didn't see it sooner. Now it's too late. No one wants to adopt an older child." No one says anything. The other children may be too shocked to speak.

"The best thing is to have your own birth parents," Janice says. "It's the only safe way. I ought to know. Two years after I was adopted, my mom gave birth to my brother. 'I wish you'd come out of me, too; I love you that much,' she's always telling me. 'I love you both the same, but he came out of me, so it's different.' How do you think that makes me feel?"

"There's no safe way. It doesn't have to do with adoption," Sylvia tells the class. She explains that she was adopted in Nicaragua by her aunt. "See, she didn't have any children, and my mom already had eight. It's not the same there as here. Children get adopted by strangers here. They never get to see their families again. I think that would be awful." Sylvia wipes at her eye. "I'm never going to see my family again either."

Someone interrupts her. "On account of your aunt moved here?"

Sylvia glares at whomever. "On account of they're all dead: my mother, my father, my sisters and brothers, my aunt and my uncle. A bomb killed them. I got adopted again and brought here. 'You must be glad to be American,' people keep telling me."

Gillian really doesn't care to hear so many sad stories. She'd probably get up and leave, except she doesn't want so much attention. That's how she comes to hear Billy's.

"A mom's not so much anyhow," he says. "Mine took off when I was a baby. My stepdad raised me, but now he's in jail, temporarily, for rape." Quite a few children sit up straighter in their chairs. "I'm staying with a foster family until he gets out. I think it could be any day now on account of his being framed." Some of the children discuss this among themselves.

"No private conversations, please. Speak up if you have something to say." It's the psychologist's job to keep them on track.

"How do you know he didn't do it?" Jeremy asks.

"See, I'm his son. Don't you think a boy knows

everything about his dad?" Billy answers, shouting. He storms from the room, knocking over a desk on his way. He doesn't come back.

After Billy's story, Gillian doesn't come back either. Nor does she mention her dropping out at home. When her aunt asks about the club, Gillian only says, "It's confidential. We're not supposed to talk about it." She watches nightly news on television instead, with her uncle, and also reads the paper. The stories there are just as bad. Sometimes Gillian takes notes or clips parts and saves them. When DeeDee asks her why, Gillian doesn't know. But all the stories have this in common: something terrible has happened to someone somewhere, and it's always more or less someone else's fault.

This happened to Erin, age four, in Florida. She was splashing at the edge of a pond with her brother, their dog, and a nine-year-old neighbor named Jason when an alligator leaped out and grabbed her. It bit her in the stomach, then pulled her underneath the water. She died from drowning. The alligator was killed later, shot five times by game wardens. Who was to blame? "The pond was a popular spot for children, even though it was full of alligators. All the kids around here played there," said the neighbors. "We've complained about the alligators before. Maybe now they'll finally do something."

Fencing in a pond can't be that hard. But what's to be done about famine? This happened in East Africa. Gillian heard a nurse from Belfast, Northern Ireland, recount it on television. The nurse said it was her worst experience. She'd gone to East Africa to help distribute food. Some baby's mother had died, and the baby needed a new mom to feed him. The nurse found him a foster mom: "Things went well for a while. The baby grew healthy and plump. Then the foster mom found out the baby was from the wrong group, people against whom her people held some long-standing grudge. She didn't give that baby back, though. No she didn't. Instead, she took that infant far away and starved him. Did not feed that child deliberately. Well," said the nurse, "I think if a mother can do this to a child, then a man can do anything to another man. I'd say seeing this made me a much harder person." Gillian thinks she wouldn't mind becoming a harder person herself. She thinks so many bad endings don't help her sleep, and also she's begun to get headaches.

That's when she turns from current events back to fairy tales. She reads them aloud to DeeDee at bedtime. Someone is always winding up dead or with her eyes plucked out.

"Can't you find something more upbeat to read?" Aunt Corinne asks her.

"Fairy tales are upbeat," Gillian answers. "The main characters all get what they deserve in the end. Everyone does. So much more fair than in real life."

This next is a favorite of hers, and she reads it enough that she knows it by heart, is glad to summarize it when asked:

THERE ONCE was a lady named Mary, so young and so fine, who fell in love with Mr. Fox. No one knew too much about him—nothing, really—not even where he lived. Lady Mary made up her mind to find out. The upshot was, she found herself exploring his castle on her own one day before their wedding. That's when she discovered Mr. Fox was a serial killer, a homicidal maniac. How else explain a room filled with skeletons of young women, all in white bridal gowns stained with blood?

You couldn't say Lady Mary hadn't been warned. There were signs everywhere in the castle. BE BOLD, BE BOLD read some. BUT NOT TOO BOLD read others. LEST THAT YOUR HEART'S BLOOD SHOULD RUN COLD cautioned the one above the door to the bridal chamber. "I think I'd best be getting home," Lady Mary told herself, backing out of that room. This was easier said than done, because just at that instant Lady Mary saw, through a window, Mr. Fox coming up the path, dragging behind him a beautiful lady in a white bridal gown who was begging and beseeching him most pitifully.

Lady Mary had time enough only to hide behind a hallway cask, when Mr. Fox came in. As he got near where Lady Mary hid, Mr. Fox noticed a diamond ring sparkling on that other lady's finger. He tried to pull it off, but when it wouldn't come, he drew his sword and hacked off that poor woman's hand at the wrist. The hand flew into the air and landed, of all places in the world, in Lady Mary's lap. Mr. Fox looked about for it but did not think to look behind the cask. At last, he continued on his way, still dragging that lady behind him. She'd fainted by now.

"I'm out of here," Lady Mary said to herself the second he was gone. She stepped from behind the cask, crept out the door, and never stopped running once until she was home.

The following day, as it happened, was the day for signing the wedding contract. It began with a splendid breakfast. When Mr. Fox was seated opposite Lady Mary, he looked at her and said, "Darling, how pale you are this morning. Is something the matter?"

"It's nothing," she answered. "Just a bad dream."

He urged her to tell it. "They say dreams go by contraries. Your sweet voice will help pass the time." Lady Mary began, describing everything she'd seen the day before as though she'd only dreamed it. Mr. Fox kept interrupting.

"Ah, but it is not so, and it was not so. And God forbid that it should be so," he said as she ticked off events, including the many signs about boldness. Lady Mary didn't contradict until the end.

Then she said, "Ah, but it is so, and it was so. Here's hand and ring I have to show," and she pulled that bloody hand, ring and all, from out of her handbag and pointed it straight at Mr. Fox. Then all the other guests stood, drew their swords, and hacked Mr. Fox into a hundred thousand pieces.

"Which was fitting," Gillian says every time she comes to the end of the story.

DeeDee likes hearing it. One thing about it confuses her. Finally, she asks. "I know Mr. Fox got what he deserved, but what about all those women? They hadn't done anything."

Gillian thinks it over, then smiles. "It depends how you look at it," she says. "See, it's a lot like a story my grandmother used to tell me, about two burros. Her story had a moral—run off with a stranger; see what you get. Don't you ever do that, DeeDee." Then Gillian tucks DeeDee in, kisses her good-night, and turns out the light. "Pleasant dreams, sleep tight," she says. But DeeDee doesn't.

"There was a monster in my room," she announces in the morning.

"It was probably just a bad dream," Gillian tells her.

"I think it's all those stories," Aunt Corinne says.

"There's nothing like a nice glass of warm milk before bed," says Uncle Henry, speaking from experience.

11

Teetering on the Edge

TENNESSEE IS hot hot hot in summertime. Iridescent lizards slip in and out beneath doors; and snakes that are or aren't dangerous, depending who you ask, crawl through grasses, slither across highways. Summer's barely started, but already Gillian is running wild. Well, wild for her; about as wild as she can run in East Tennessee, still a preteen with no car—hitching rides, hanging out, barelegged, in sneakers, printed-on T-shirts, torn jeans, and no underwear. What would her grandmother say if she could see Gillian now? Probably say, it's a good thing she's not in New York. But Gillian's grandmother says that already.

She sees every day what goes on there, taking subways back and forth to work and school, early mornings and evenings, out on the streets, running. Wherever she goes, it's the same: garbage-strewn sidewalks, boarded-up buildings, homeless people living in doorways, teenage mothers on crack and their babies, smells of urine in elevators and hallways, used condoms and needles lying in school yards, and always some grown person reaching out a hand to help someone young into trouble.

It isn't like that in Oak Ridge. Parents love raising children there; so much open space and fresh air; so much harder there for a child to go wrong. Even a child looking for trouble might have to go a distance to find it, and then might wind up finding something else instead. In years to come, when Gillian looks back at this time in her life, she'll recall it this way: "It was just a feeling that I had, as though I couldn't stay still. Every second I spent by myself, I felt about to jump out of my skin. It was as if my skin had grown too tight for me." *Too light* is my own interpretation, because when I think of Gillian that summer, I see her reaching out toward darkness, the familiarity of color, comforting reminders of home—somewhere black to relieve the oppressive, unnatural, not-counting-her, absolute whiteness of where she now found herself.

Gillian turns out lucky, but the moral is, she didn't have to. She knows of only two places to go, both near the turnpike—Time Out Deli, where she first ate with

Aunt Corinne and DeeDee, and Mr. Dixon's auto body shop, where she did her interview for school. She can get to either one by putting up her thumb, and she does. Of course it's dangerous, plus there's no telling what she'll find at the end of the ride.

Except, I know this: a certain group of friends hangs out in both places; count Lily and Donny, Charelle and Janeen, Tony and Tyler, Elijah and Jackson, for starters. They're all from that section of Oak Ridge called Scarboro, and older than Gillian, say high school age. Maybe one or two have dropped out. Another few work part-time in the deli after school, weekends, and during summer vacation. Lily, for instance, who right away takes Gillian under her wing, insists on fixing her oversize subs, summer hoagies with extra cheese, telling her as she does, "Girl, you need to put some meat on your bones—eat!" Then, when her shift is over, Lily gathers her things, and Gillian, and together they walk the few blocks to Mr. Dixon's.

There's a good chance the others already are there. Mr. Dixon is used to a full house, Scarboro children hanging out. He doesn't mind. He figures as long as they're with him, they're keeping out of trouble. He makes no difference between boys and girls. He puts them all to work—hand-washing cars, going for parts, cleaning up. "Who knows, one of you may wind up an auto mechanic or engineer. Keep your eyes on the future," he tells them.

"Hey there, New York. What's happening?" he says when he sees Gillian. "Your uncle know you're here?" he asks after the first few times. He thinks she's kind of young to be hanging out on her own so much of the time. He also knows she's not from Scarboro. Gillian looks at the ground, moves her lips, says something. It could be yes or no. Mr. Dixon makes up his mind to ask about her the next time he sees Henry. But he doesn't for some weeks, and then only because of a conversation he overhears between Gillian and Lily:

"Say what? You get around how? What's wrong with you, girl? Don't you ever listen to your television? You'd better start paying attention. All the time it's telling you about this crazy person or that one, all of them out there, just waiting for some kind of fool. You'd better not be that fool. Next time I hear about you hitching any more rides, I'm gonna have a talk with your aunt. You want to go someplace, you call me or Tony or Jackson here. Some one of us'll come get you or find you a ride."

And they would if they had to. It's already mid-July. They've begun to think of Gillian as a baby sister; treat her like one, too. They tease her.

"You're so skinny, you walk by the graveyard

someone be taking you for a skeleton. Have some fries."

"They be taking her for a ghost is what they be taking her for. New York, if I were you, I'd sit out in that sun like whitefolks do, and get me some tan."

"You quit bothering that child," Lily says, jumping in. "Think you're so smart. You don't know nothing. That's how you're supposed to look when you're from the Islands. You're just jealous on account of Gillian looks so good." It's almost as though Lily's gone and adopted her. Listening, Mr. Dixon smiles. He knows Gillian's in good hands, but still he thinks her transportation should be someone else's problem. He makes arrangements to talk it over with her uncle.

That's how come the third week in July finds both men sitting over tall glasses of iced tea at the boardwalk restaurant by the lake, discussing Gillian. Precisely what they say is anyone's guess, but when Henry Hardwick gets home that night, he tells his wife this, or something like it:

"At least we know where Gillian goes when she's gone, and it's safe." He hopes it's the truth even as he says it. "Well, not counting the transportation part," he adds. By morning, they've come up with a plan. From now on, Gillian will ride downtown with her aunt every day after lunch when she goes to work. Downtown isn't that big. Gillian can walk wherever she likes. The deli is less than five blocks from the library; Mr. Dixon's garage isn't much farther. Uncle Henry will pick her up on his way home. Such a simple solution. Yet Gillian doesn't look happy.

Every day, from now on, her aunt and uncle watch as she goes to and fro from the car, moving slowly, as though carrying the weight of the world on her thin shoulders, with no way to set it down. Of course they worry. This sorrow-eyed, amber-skinned child is their niece, after all, dressed as she is in tight jeans with nothing on underneath. It doesn't take a sharp eye to notice. So why hasn't anyone mentioned it?

Well, I'm sure they have, just not to Gillian. At least, not yet. But it's not hard to picture Aunt Corinne on the phone, talking to whomever: "If I had to guess, I'd say some sort of political statement, or maybe just her way of expressing herself, asserting her freedom. You know how girls can be at that age."

I know she doesn't say this to Gillian's grandmother, because I know what she'd say. Of course, she'd be thinking of someone in a skirt when she said it. "Free? How free can a person be who can't even bend over because everyone will see what she has?"

Or, in Gillian's case, doesn't have. Still no hair down there, for instance, or anywhere but on her head. Nor any other signs of oncoming puberty. Even in her T-shirt and jeans, that much is obvious. It may be the point. A girl like that isn't so likely to get into trouble. I'd say it goes a long way toward explaining so many stories I've heard of pure and pantie-less girls. This is just one of them, from Singapore.

There were two schools, side by side, one for boys and one for girls. Both were Catholic, with nuns for teachers. One day, some of the boys hung a kite in a tree alongside the fence dividing the play yards. A little girl climbed the fence to get the kite. But the boys had tricked her. They all stood by the fence, laughing and pointing. They could see that little girl's underpants.

She climbed down right away, shamefaced and kiteless. Every girl in that play yard had witnessed what had happened to her. She was publicly mortified. Then that little girl's best friend secretly took off her own pair of underpants and put it into her pocket. When lunchtime came and the nuns were busy elsewhere, she climbed the fence just as she was, and calmly took down the kite. The same boys looked up, jeering, and then there was total silence. They could not believe what they saw. They had no words for it. They were speechless.

This next story also is true. It's about a girl I once knew who became a nun. Gillian's grandmother knew her, too. But before that girl was a nun, she was a wild child, believe me. She ran around scantily clad, in tight skirts "up to her gazoos," as we said then, probably with nothing more on underneath than a garter belt to hold up her nylons. Panty hose was just starting to come in. She smoked unfiltered cigarettes, was known to drink whiskey, and danced "the fish" with guys to slow music at parties where parents weren't at home. She rode behind boyfriends on their motorcycles, and up front on their bicycle handlebars. In those days, that was really something. Mothers held her up to their daughters as an example. "See, she's boy-crazy. Don't you be that way," they'd say.

She had a twin brother who was even wilder. Eventually, and for a few years, he became an autocar racer. Afterward, he married his high school sweetheart, settled down, and had children. He bought an auto supply store and did very well. People who knew him from before would say, "See, he got all his wildness out of his system while he was still young."

While she was still young, his sister became a nun. She would have become one sooner, but her parents insisted she wait at least until she finished high school. Then they threw her a big party, during which they weren't at home. It was called as both a graduation and a going-away-to-the-convent celebration. It lasted a whole weekend. Her parents allowed it because they kept hoping she would change her mind. They couldn't understand why she wanted to go into a convent. But I believe it was because she saw it as the only way to save herself from her own wildness. "If I do this, then I won't do that," she must have told herself.

When I consider Gillian's state of dress that summer, in a peculiar way I see her motivation as similar. Pantie-less, she would have known exactly what part of her most needed protection. Also, there's this: the same as the girl in the school yard or Lady Mary in the story, Gillian may simply have understood all along the advantage of boldness.

Not that I overlook weather completely. Summertime in Tennessee—you can imagine how hot. Looking back, Gillian will say, "Even the air stuck to me. Every single thing that I put on seemed so confining. I think I would have gone naked if I could. I felt grateful every night just to see the sun go down."

THE SUN SETS late in East Tennessee, situated as it is at the westernmost end of its time zone. Gillian, like any person used to city lights, is astonished by the overwhelming darkness of starless, moonless nights; and equally amazed by the night sky's brilliance when stars appear and the moon is full. She never quite gets used to how many tiny green bugs, whose name she never learns, flood inside the house the second she opens an outside door without remembering first to turn off every single inside light. Nor does she ever become entirely accustomed to so many night noises —frogs, insects, and birds. One thing, though: however freely Gillian runs around in the daytime, she's home at night.

Well, where could she go in Tennessee after dark at her age? Or any age, really? There's not a whole lot to do. There are some movie houses, and every now and then Aunt Corinne and Uncle Henry drive to one in Knoxville, leaving both girls at home, with Gillian in charge. Gillian looks forward to these evenings, and it's for them that she prevails upon Lily to buy her cigarettes. Underage as Gillian is, and looking even younger than her years, she'd have a hard time trying to buy them on her own. Still, Lily doesn't like it.

"You shouldn't be smoking. Didn't you ever hear of lung cancer?" she asks.

"Ain't gonna smoke them," Gillian tells her.

"Well, just so as you don't burn your house down either," Lily says, frowning. She worries she's doing the wrong thing, but she also remembers being Gillian's age herself, and helpless.

Gillian does neither. Her sole purpose in obtaining cigarettes is to enable her to pursue her new hobby; she's practicing art, developing her own form of collage. For this, she also needs photographs. Fortunately, DeeDee has an instant camera with a flash, a birthday gift from her parents last year. She loves taking pictures of Gillian.

Gillian sometimes dresses up for their photo sessions; drapes herself, for instance, in the paisley shawl that belonged to her mother, or wears one of Uncle Henry's straw hats, or one of his caps, or his work boots. Other times, she removes articles of her own clothing instead; or pulls something up or down, exposing this or that part of her body. Afterward, she cuts the photographs into pieces and pastes them onto sheets of construction paper, with her body parts rearranged. An arm may be sticking up from her head, for instance. Or parts may be missing; a leg stretched out by itself, perhaps, on a bed Gillian has penciled in as part of the background or drawn with colored chalks. More than once, she has pulled over a chair, sat in front of the hallway mirror, and sketched a self-portrait. Sometimes, she gives herself birthmarks or tattoos. These pictures, too, she cuts up, or else pastes over them portions of snapshots, or torn pictures she's taken from old magazines, or the stories she once clipped from newspapers and saved. Just when she seems to be finished, she will take out a cigarette and light it. Then, as DeeDee stares in awful fascination, Gillian begins burning holes in her work.

"Why are you doing that?" DeeDee asks.

"It's art," Gillian tells her. But years later, she'll say, "A psychiatrist would probably conclude I was trying to hurt myself symbolically. That's not my recollection. I think I was trying to strengthen myself, as though in this way I could make myself invulnerable."

Of course, that's not possible, as one can tell just from looking at a photo. Naturally, DeeDee's aren't the only ones in the house. Some of the others are also recent. Gillian doesn't bother with these, doesn't even think about burning holes in them. There's this one, for instance: DeeDee, Gillian, and Aunt Corinne are seated in a rowboat, surrounded by water. DeeDee and her mom are in the middle, their backs to the camera, each with an oar in one hand. They're smiling over their shoulders into the lens. Gillian is gingerly perched on the farthest seat, at the wide end of the boat, already facing the camera. Her expression is guarded, and it's not hard to guess she'd rather be someplace else—anyplace, other than here.

It was Uncle Henry who took the picture. He'd borrowed the boat one Sunday in June from someone at work. I can just see him standing there in shallow water, his swimming trunks on, trying hard to keep the camera dry. "Smile, everyone," he must have said; then waited until, finally, when it was clear Gillian wasn't about to, he'd snapped the picture anyway and climbed into the boat. Then they'd all put on life jackets and, not counting Gillian, taken turns rowing. Afterward, they'd come back to the dock, tied up the boat, and picnicked at a long wooden table, cold hamburgers on buttered rolls from home and warm soda pop. Gillian was past being surprised by the menu. What she remembers most about that day were so many mosquitoes.

What DeeDee remembers most was how much fun they all had. She likes to take out the picture and discuss it. She does so now, this evening, when all four of them are together in the house, the television on. She hands the snapshot to her father.

"If Mommie, Gillian, and I were all in a boat, and the boat overturned, who would you save?" she asks him. If her father is startled by her question, he doesn't show it.

"I'd save Gillian," he says, without blinking. "You and Mommie know how to swim." It's true: Gillian is the only one in the room who doesn't.

"CAN'T SWIM?" Lily is surprised the next day to hear it. She and Gillian are standing outside the garage, along with some others, gabbing.

"And you coming from the Islands, too," Donny marvels.

"New York Island, stupid," Charelle says. "It's not the same. Where's she gonna swim in New York?" They all know how to swim, having taken lessons years ago at the outdoor town pool. People boasted then about how it was filled with natural spring water. Now there is talk of closing it down because of contamination. They discuss the subject among themselves, but

Gillian isn't listening. She's daydreaming about swimming in New York. She pictures the East River, the Hudson; she knows there are Y's in the city with indoor pools.

"When I was your age," Gillian's grandmother used to tell her, "grown-ups warned us, 'If you swim in the river, you'll die.' We believed just dipping our toes in would kill us. Well, who knows? It probably would have. Even pools could be dangerous. Every summer there were stories in the newspapers about children who'd cracked open their skulls, hitting their heads together, diving. But, of course, the main fear was polio."

Gillian already knew about polio. Her grandmother had a friend who'd had it. Although she'd recovered, afterward one of her legs was shorter than the other.

"It evens out in the end," she used to joke. "One leg is shorter, but the other one's longer." Some time ago, she stopped joking. As she got older, the effects of her polio started coming back. Increasingly, she had difficulty walking, sometimes even breathing. She had to go back to wearing leg braces. "My greatest fear," she said, "is needing an iron lung again."

"Don't worry," Gillian's grandmother told her. "You won't, and even if you ever did, I'm sure they make them better nowadays, lighter weight, probably portable." Her friend wasn't consoled, but Gillian, when she recalls that conversation now, for one split second smiles. Then she wipes at one eye. In her head, she sees her grandmother, in training, running down a street somewhere in Queens, say along Union Turnpike, breathing easily as she goes, her mind free of all care. "When you're running, there isn't room for anything else in your head." Isn't that what she'd said? Gillian's own breathing becomes suddenly labored. She feels as though a weight is pressing on her heart. She kicks at the ground with one foot, stirring up gravel: How stupid can I be even to think about Grandma? Why should I care? One thing's for sure; she's not thinking of me.

A few days later, though, Gillian takes up running herself, just now and then. On some late afternoon or early evening, you can see her in cutoff jeans, an old T-shirt, and new running shoes, sprinting coltlike on slim legs around the track outside the Civic Center. Not too many others are using it. It's August, after all—so much heat.

Lily sometimes comes by just to watch. She herself doesn't think much of running in circles. "Don't you get bored?" she asks Gillian.

"Umm-hmm," Gillian answers. "But it's still better than the highway—much safer. At least I've never seen a single naked man here." She's referring, of course, to her first Tennessee spring, when she went looking for wildflowers. She doesn't plan to run into another undressed man if she can help it, or that same one.

"I see," says Lily. Then she adds, "You need to be wearing more clothing yourself. A person first meeting you could get the wrong idea." She means Gillian should have on something underneath her T-shirt and shorts. "Running around the way that you are is only asking for trouble."

I don't blame Lily for thinking that. I've thought it myself, and not only about Gillian. I've watched her grandmother run around, too; and I don't mean just training. I think any person, seeing those two this summer, might wonder at the restless pace they've set themselves, their frenzied movement, so much wasted energy. Even standing still, they seem perpetually in motion.

"See, they're running amok," a person might say, but not me. I see, instead, a girl and her grandmother, each teetering separately on some imaginary ledge, in trouble and mourning. I remember what Darlene once said, the girl whose mother died from bone cancer. She said it to Gillian's mother, who told it to *her* mother, who told it to me.

"After my mother died, I thought that I would lose my mind. I couldn't believe how angry at her I was, or that I could miss her so much. I felt I was having a nervous breakdown. After a while, I got over it." I was glad for Darlene.

Recalling her now, I ask myself, will Gillian and her grandmother get over it, too? Will something, or someone, come along to cause them to step back from the edge? And if so, what, or who, could it be?

In Gillian's case, I'd say thank goodness for Antoine.

12

Antoine

ANTOINE'S VISIT came the last ten days in August. The week before, it was nearly all DeeDee talked about. He was on his way from Hawaii, where his father was stationed in the military, to Colorado, to start college at the Air Force Academy.

"Besides you, he's my only cousin. Of course, he's your cousin, too," DeeDee informed Gillian happily.

"He isn't *my* cousin," Gillian said. "He's your mother's sister's child. It's a whole different side of the family." Being older, Gillian understood genealogy better. Nevertheless, when Antoine arrived, she was more than a little surprised.

I wonder how come no one ever mentioned his being Chinese, she wondered. Or maybe his father is. Or Vietnamese. Or Korean. If there was some way to tell the difference, Gillian didn't know it. Of course, if her aunt and uncle were the sort to frame photographs and hang them on walls or prop them on tables, instead of sticking them into drawers and closets as soon as they got them, Gillian might have seen one of Antoine and asked questions.

This one, for instance—an eight-by-ten glossy, taken not *that* long ago, obviously on some formal occasion, a sophomore school dance, perhaps, or somebody's wedding. It's mixed in with other photos beneath a stack of linen napkins in the dining room china cabinet. This is how Antoine looks in it: he is seated in a leather wing chair, wearing a black tuxedo. A white carnation is pinned to the collar. His shirt cuffs peek out from beneath the jacket sleeves, and his hands are clasped gracefully at his waist, hiding most of the cummerbund. He has thick black hair. A few strands in front are sticking straight up, and one wisp has fallen, or perhaps been placed, in a curl on his forehead. His eyebrows are dark and distinctly arched above bright almond-shaped eyes. He seems to be gazing directly at the viewer. His mouth is full and sensuous, with a faint shadow above his upper lip. He isn't smiling; yet the prominence of his cheekbones is obvious. They are high and wide set. His skin is flawless, olive in tone. The first time I ever saw this picture, I envisioned Mongolian conquerors, who swept across China and Europe centuries ago and left behind such romantic good looks as part of their legacy.

If Antoine were suddenly to smile, stand, and step out from his picture, you'd notice this, too, about him: enchanting, long dimples, one in each cheek, and perfect teeth. He's also relatively short and slightly built. Not more than five foot six, I think. Gillian is nearly as tall already, and she still has inches to grow. It's no wonder she was surprised when she saw Antoine actually standing there in front of her. He certainly didn't look like the rest of the family.

"How come you never mentioned about your cousin being Asian?" Gillian asked DeeDee the first chance she got. They were outside, sitting on the doorstep, hitting at mosquitoes. The usual nighttime racket was going on, the relentless clamor of Tennessee wildlife.

"Antoine isn't Asian, silly. He's American like us. He's just adopted."

"I see," Gillian said, and dropped the topic. The next time she brought it up was alone with Antoine.

"So, I guess we have some things in common," she said. She couldn't very well start out by saying, "I hear you're adopted." Antoine flashed his smile at her.

"Sure we do. We've got the same family." Gillian studied him carefully. He appeared to be serious.

"That's not what I mean. I mean we're in the

same boat. Our ancestors came from someplace not Europe, and we don't look the same as the people we live with. Plus we don't have real parents."

"I have real parents," Antoine said. He was no longer smiling, but his tone was gentle. Gillian momentarily looked confused.

"Yes, well, but you're adopted. It's almost the same."

"I don't look at it that way," Antoine told her.

Gillian seemed to think this over. Maybe she was remembering Wayne from her Banana Splits club, first adopted, then returned. Or Janice, who'd believed having one's own birth parents was the only safe way. But, then, it turned out it wasn't.

"So, how do you look at it?" Gillian asked.

"I look at it that I'm lucky having my mom and dad that I do."

"Sure, but wouldn't you rather they looked Chinese like you?" Of course, it was still possible his father did, but Antoine just laughed at her.

"Try Filipino. The Philippines is where I was born."

Gillian considered this. Her expression brightened. "See, I was right. We have Island ancestors in common. I was just wrong about them all being on the same boat. My great-grandmother came here with her mom from Trinidad when she was three. My grandmother was the first one of us born here. She's a runner now, and in school, but as soon as she settles down, I'm going back to New York to live with her."

It was after this conversation Gillian took to following Antoine around, asking more questions or sometimes the same ones again. It isn't prying, she told herself. I'm only trying to find out.

"Tell the truth. Don't you ever mind looking so different from your folks? Like, for instance, when you go places together and people stare?"

"I don't pay attention. Unless someone brings it up, it isn't anything I think about." Well, Antoine could say that, but probably living on military bases has helped, not to mention Hawaii, where people have a more international outlook. Gillian persisted.

"Maybe not now. But what about before, say when you were two or three; like the day you looked in a mirror and for the first time really noticed."

"When I was three, I was still in the orphanage," Antoine told her. "I was six when I was adopted. Believe me, I was so glad to be leaving, how anybody looked was the last thing on my mind. What I minded was my new mom could speak only English. I spoke Tagalog. Communicating was tricky."

"What did you do?"

"I learned English fast."

Gillian sat quietly for a minute or two. It was a lot to absorb. She had to organize her feelings. Then she asked, "Did something terrible happen to your birth parents? Did they die? Were they in some kind of accident?"

"Not that I know. Of course, I've been gone from the Philippines a long time. Anything's possible. But, see, I try to keep that whole side of my life out of my mind. I like to think of starting out for the first time the day my mom and Aunt Corinne came and got me."

"Aunt Corinne?" Gillian was as amazed as she had ever been. "Why didn't your father come instead?"

"He was busy. He'd just been transferred from Clark Air Base in the Philippines to Thailand. My mom was already back in the States when she got the news I was available. The way I've heard it, my mom telephoned Aunt Corinne. 'If we hurry,' she told her, 'I can bring home a little boy.' So that's what they did. My mom hates flying. She didn't want to go alone."

Some things are beyond imagining. Gillian tried hard but couldn't begin to put herself in Antoine's place, at age six, with no parents, ever, to call his own or even a single person to count on, simply for being there, say tomorrow, and the next day, and the day after that. Of course, now Gillian was a child without parents herself, but once she'd had some, and she still did have her grandmother. Gillian couldn't begin to think how Antoine had survived. She asked him.

"I just did. I prayed a lot. Every night, and even

in the daytime, I prayed for a mother to come get me. When mine did, I knew my prayers had been answered. At first, I worried she might send me back. Then I'd think how far we'd come, how long the trip had taken, and I decided probably she wouldn't. It was a lot of stress for a six-year-old. I had tantrums. Each time one was over, I felt so relieved to find out they were still planning to keep me.

"But as you can see, things turned out fine. Before a year was up, I went to school, spoke English like a regular American, and was adjusted." Antoine laughed. "Mostly adjusted. Once, in second grade, my class was discussing nationality. 'I used to be Filipino. I'm American now,' I announced, standing. 'When I grow up, my children will be American, too. But their friends will speak Chinese.'

"Naturally, I meant speak Tagalog. I figured none of the other children had heard of it, though. Maybe not even the teacher. See, I was trying not to stand out. 'Thank you, Antoine, for sharing,' the teacher said. 'Please take your seat. Let's hope you'll remember to raise your hand the next time you have something to say to the class.'"

ANTOINE'S TENNESSEE visit passed by fast. I wouldn't say he upset the family routine, only changed it. Most days, for instance, he dropped Aunt Corinne off at the library, so that he could have the use of her car. Later, he, or sometimes Uncle Henry, picked her up.

On Aunt Corinne's day off, Antoine accompanied her to the raptor center, where he photographed predatory birds and helped feed them. "No, thank you," Gillian said when invited. "I think I'll stay home and wash my hair."

Sometimes, Antoine dropped Gillian off, too—at the deli or auto body shop—or picked her up.

"Hey, there, good-looking!" Lily teased him.

"You've got yourself a fine cousin. You look after him now," Mr. Dixon told Gillian.

"Thank you," Gillian said; then, in the interest of truthfulness, added, "Well, he isn't really my cousin."

Most of the time, though, Gillian tagged along where Antoine went, sight-seeing: to the zoo in Knoxville, the Museum of Appalachia, Great Smoky Mountains National Park.

DeeDee complained: "It isn't fair. He's my cousin, too. Why do I have to go to camp every day, and Gillian gets to go everywhere with him?"

"Gillian's older." It wasn't an answer DeeDee cared to hear.

Gillian and Antoine's farthest, and final, excursion took them three hours southwest to tour a whiskey distillery, Jack Daniel, located in a county that was dry. Afterward, they bought sparkling white grape juice in the souvenir shop, then started home in a downpour. If not for the weather, Gillian might never have heard such shocking news as she did about Uncle Henry, and also her father. It started out with a conversation about Aunt Corinne. Antoine had pulled off the road to wait for the rain to let up.

"If we had a car phone, we could telephone Aunt Corinne—tell her we'll be late, not to wait for us for dinner. That way, she wouldn't worry."

Gillian shrugged, wiped perspiration from her lip. "Who cares if she does?"

"I do," said Antoine. Gillian made a face.

"I don't," she said. "If not for my uncle, I wouldn't be living here in the first place. She's not my real aunt. I never picked her. She's only the person Uncle Henry married. I get so tired always trying to please her. Don't get me wrong. It's not that I dislike her. I just don't see where we have anything in common." Gillian had kept these thoughts inside so long, it felt good getting them out. She certainly never expected Antoine to take them personally, or to close his eyes and lean his forehead against the steering wheel, as he did now. I guess you could say he was collecting his thoughts.

Having done so, he raised his head, looked at Gillian, and said, "In case you haven't noticed, we don't get to pick a whole lot in this life, and certainly not when it comes to relatives. One thing you can say for Aunt Corinne, at least she tries. She never picked me to be her nephew, but since the day my mom adopted me, she's been my aunt."

"Well, sure," Gillian said lamely. "See, that gave you something in common."

Antoine sighed. I would have, too. How could it be, one human being, two human beings, and nothing in common?

"Your trouble is, you can't stop feeling sorry for yourself," Antoine told her, without sounding angry. "Well, it's understandable; your life hasn't been easy. You have to get over it. People do, you know; otherwise they'd never get on with their lives. Just look at Uncle Henry."

"Uncle Henry?" said Gillian.

"Sure," said Antoine. "Now his childhood was really hard, but he got over it."

"Hard how?" Gillian asked. So Antoine told her the parts that he knew.

"UNCLE HENRY was four, and your father had just been born, when *their* father died," Antoine said. "Until that point, I guess it was a pretty good life. Their father was a traveling salesman, on his way home, less than six miles away, when a drunk driver's car jumped the divider, ran into his, and killed him. So then the boys were fatherless and also very poor. Two years later, their mother remarried, a warrant officer in the army. He was okay sober, but often he was drunk. Those times he beat his wife and sometimes both boys. Henry thought it was his job to protect them. He tried, but of course he couldn't. He was only six. They lived that way, scared, for three years.

"Finally, when Henry was nine and your father was five, their stepfather came home early one day, drunk and reeling. Henry was doing homework at the kitchen table, and your father was finger-painting. Their mother was sitting beside them, watching. Her hand was in her pocket. She took out a gun. Who knows where she got it? She aimed it at her husband and shot him. Both boys looked on as she did. The first shot killed him. She shot five more times to be sure. That's what Henry told the police, confirming his mother's version.

"There was blood, and also finger paint, everywhere. Eventually, there was a trial, after which their mother was confined to an asylum for the criminally insane. The boys were sent to live with their grandmother, their mother's mother. Every few months, they would visit their mother in the asylum. Afterward, your father would behave like a crazy person himself, hoping to be sent there to live with her. He wasn't, but by then their grandmother, who was old and in poor health, had decided the boys were too much of a handful for her. They were placed in a home for nondelinquent children in need of protection. Later, they were shuttled from one foster family to another.

"After a while, their grandmother died. Then, their mother died, too. She was still in the asylum. The boys hadn't seen her in a long time. Maybe she died from grief, or was killed by some other patient, or given a wrong injection, or caught pneumonia. Who knows why? The boys were on their own. Well, Uncle Henry was on his own. He was about sixteen at the time. But your father lived, as he always had, under his brother's protection, which I understand was considerable. Now that was a hard life," Antoine said. "But, see, Uncle Henry didn't let it get him down. He turned out fine. He always kept a positive attitude, and so should you. It's the only way to get by."

ANTOINE stopped speaking. I can just see the two of them sitting there, sticky, in such a hot car, on that rain-drenching day late in August. Such close quarters, the glass all fogged up from just two people's breathing. Even before the rain had fully ended, they'd rolled down the windows. You can imagine how little that helped, hot and humid as it was, everywhere dripping. You can imagine the sounds, too, shrill and raucous, put forth by Tennessee fauna heartened by so much new moisture. Add to that the *swish-swish-hums* of passing vehicles as traffic picked up on the highway. I can just hear Gillian ask her question.

"You wouldn't happen to know if Uncle Henry or my father got to see their mother after she was dead?"

How hard Antoine must have stared. Surely, this was not a question he had been expecting. "Did they what?" he asked finally.

"Did they see their mother dead?" Gillian persisted. "I never saw mine. She was buried before I ever got back to New York. It was a private ceremony. Only my grandmother was there. I never got to tell my mom good-bye."

Antoine shook his head. "That's something you'd have to ask Uncle Henry. It's not a topic anyone discusses with me. I only know what I do from listening. You could call it a survival skill I picked up in the orphanage." Antoine started the car. Then, heading northeast, he took his right hand from the steering wheel, reached out, and squeezed Gillian's shoulder. Gillian smiled. It lit up her face.

THE NEXT DAY was Antoine's last full one in Tennessee. He spent most of it packing, confirming reservations, attending to final details. Gillian spent most of it hanging around watching, trying not to get in the way. This happened after dinner, which was late—spaghetti with canned sauce and meatballs. Uncle Henry was carrying plates to the sink when Antoine made his announcement: "I think we should

[147]

have a memorial service for Gillian's mom before I leave. It will be a year since she died this Christmas, but I'll be back home in Hawaii. So I say let's do it now while all five of us are present."

Four of the five I'm sure were surprised, but no one said no. Only Uncle Henry said, "Just wait a minute, though, while I finish clearing the table. That's better," he said, taking his seat.

ANTOINE BEGAN, head bowed, his lips compressed into a thin, straight line, elongating his dimples. He placed both elbows on the tabletop, entwined his fingers, and rested his chin on the ridge of his knuckles. Seeing him that way, so serious, made the others sit up straighter and look more serious, too. Even DeeDee, who another time might have giggled, was solemn.

"We are gathered here this evening to hold a memorial service for Gillian's mom, who died too young and who will always be missed," Antoine intoned. "We will go around the table and each say something good we remember about her. I will go first. I never met Gillian's mom myself, but I think she must have been a very special person because she raised Gillian to be special, too, and I know she loved Gillian very much. I am sorry I never met her; yet I feel that I knew her, because what was best in her is also present in Gillian."

Then it was Uncle Henry's turn. "Gillian's mom

loved Gillian. She was a good person who worked hard and always tried her best. Often, her life wasn't easy, but she always looked on the bright side. She was a good teacher, a good actress, and a wonderful singer. I think God must have loved her very much to have given her so much talent, and also to have given her Gillian. We wish she could have stayed on earth with us longer, but since she couldn't, we are grateful to Gillian's grandmother for sending Gillian here to us, for sharing her beloved granddaughter." It was a lot for Uncle Henry to say, but then, I think, isn't that what eloquence is, an expression of the heart?

Aunt Corinne went next. She'd only met Gillian's mom once before she got sick, at her own wedding. She knew her mostly from the little Uncle Henry had told her, plus telephone calls and letters. "Gillian's mom was a beautiful person," Aunt Corinne said. "She was beautiful on the outside and on the inside. She was so thrilled whenever Gillian learned something new. 'My child is the cleverest child in the world,' she'd say when Gillian was a baby, calling to tell us. I loved hearing her voice on the telephone. I loved getting her letters, written in different colors of ink. She was always so proud of you, Gillian. We're proud of you, too,"

It was DeeDee's turn. Antoine encouraged her. "Go ahead, even if you can think of only one thing."

"I wish I had known Gillian's mom better,"

DeeDee said. "I think she is in heaven now, looking down on Gillian. She must miss Gillian a lot. God bless Gillian's mom, and God bless Gillian. God bless Gillian's grandmother, too," she added.

Gillian was last. "I miss my mom. She was a very good mom to me. She loved me and cared what I did. I always believed, so long as she was with me, nothing bad could ever happen to me. Even at the end, I thought that. I never believed she'd really die." Gillian faltered.

"I guess that's about it," Antoine said. He unclasped his hands to show the memorial service was at its end. "We will always remember Gillian's mom and miss her. She was a good person and loved Gillian very much. So do we all—Uncle Henry, Aunt Corinne, DeeDee and I, and Gillian's grandmother. Amen." Everyone else said amen, too. Gillian was surprised to find she actually felt better.

"Thank you," she said to Antoine, before going to bed.

LATE THE NEXT AFTERNOON, when Uncle Henry, Aunt Corinne, and DeeDee took Antoine to the airport, Gillian stayed home.

"I'd rather say good-bye here," she told him. I'm sure that was true, but I think not her only reason. My guess is she also wanted time alone, the house to herself, some privacy; and why not? Wouldn't anyone in Gillian's position need to take a step backward, look closely at herself, sort out her innermost thoughts and her feelings?

Of course, it's just my opinion. Nevertheless, when I think of Gillian that evening, alone in the house, this is how I picture her: she is standing in the larger of the two bathrooms, undressed for her shower, examining herself in front of the full-length mirror that hangs inside on the door. She turns her slim body this way and that, looking for signs that are unmistakable. She fingers the two soft new bumps pushing up on either side of her chest, where before only tiny nipples had barely protruded. She lightly strokes, with the tip of one thumb, the few stray hairs here and there, nowhere profuse enough to offer cover. Her body's outline is still a child's, but some parts show new definition—her hips, for instance, and her buttocks.

She bends forward slowly, her eyes still on the mirror, runs her hands up and down both legs, testing. *Wild women shave!* How often she'd heard her mother and her grandmother tell that to each other, meaning those same women they talked about who stood on street corners and did goodness knows what and with whom. *Well, whitewomen shave, too,* said in tones of pity. *But they have to. Whitepeople are so hairy.* Gillian knows that it's true. She's never gotten over her amazement, in this house of closed doors and hidden body parts, at hearing Aunt Corinne announce at breakfast, "Well, I guess I'd better go shave my legs"; or her asking Uncle Henry to pick up razor blades for her on his way home. Relieved at her own legs' smoothness, Gillian steps back from the mirror, turns on the shower, and steps in.

So much cool water is soothing. She anoints herself with almond-scented suds, soap ordered from a catalog, one of Aunt Corinne's few overtures to luxury. Gillian rinses, then turns off the water, steps out, wraps herself all around in a thick wine-colored bath towel, and, almost dry, slips into a cool cotton nightgown, a gift last spring from her grandmother—pale green, and so soft it could be cotton batting she's put on. She pads barefoot to her room, takes her photo album from the bookcase, and looks through it for the first time since her mother died. She stares hard at pictures of her mother, her grandmother, herself, and, also, at the single snapshot she has of both her parents together. When she's finished looking, she closes the album and replaces it. The rose quartz Island stone on top of the bookcase catches her eye. She picks it up, holds it cupped in her hand, smiles as she thinks of Aunt Sylvia and Grandma. Then she puts the stone down and, still barefoot, walks down the hallway to use the telephone in Aunt Corinne and Uncle Henry's room.

THAT'S WHEN she called her grandmother collect; though she knew she didn't have to, knew that no one would mind her dialing direct; knew, too, if she waited, her grandmother would call her in the morning, like clockwork, never having missed a single last Sunday in the month since Gillian first came here to live, even the time her grandmother was out of the country, running in Italy, and Gillian's mother was in Tennessee with her.

"Hi! It's me, Gillian," she said, hearing her grandmother answer the phone.

"Yes, I know." Her grandmother accepted the call, sounded glad to hear Gillian. Has she ever sounded any other way?

"So, how are you doing?"

"I'm fine. How are you?"

"I'm fine, too. Well, I miss you. Antoine and everyone's gone to the airport."

"I miss you, too. But you know I'm coming to see you at Christmas. You'll probably be so grown by then, I won't know you."

Gillian giggled. "Aunt Corinne's taking DeeDee and me shopping for school clothes on Monday, as much as you can shop in Tennessee. I've about outgrown everything I have."

"Is there something in particular you need me to send?" Gillian didn't answer right away. "Are you there?" her grandmother asked. It was long distance, after all.

"I'm thinking. I guess I could use new underwear;

underpants, but don't think I still wear undershirts.
I'm not a baby anymore, you know. If bras come in
small, that's probably my size. I don't know how to
buy them. . . ."

LESS THAN A WEEK after this conversation,
a box arrived for Gillian, containing half a dozen
white cotton bras in two sizes, the smallest cup so
flat even Gillian had no trouble wearing it; a dozen
pairs of assorted pastel-colored panties; several half-
slips, and one full one, in white cotton lawn trimmed
with lace. There were, besides, three small packages,
each gift wrapped and labeled. I know what they
contained: a jar of guava jam for Aunt Corinne and
Uncle Henry; a navy sweatshirt with a picture on it of
a large red dog, for DeeDee; and a pen and pencil set,
to be sent to Antoine. Also enclosed for Gillian were
a letter and a pamphlet. The pamphlet was titled
"Becoming a Woman." It explained menstruation. I
can just see Gillian smile. Hadn't her mother already
told her everything she'd need to know? And even if
she hadn't, didn't Gillian have Lily? Gillian read the
letter.

Dear Gillian,
I hope everything fits, and if not now, then
soon. I hope you are being good and not causing
your relatives any problems. I want you to

concentrate on schoolwork and not worry about a social life. I will tell you when it's time to think about boys. Give my best regards to your uncle and aunt, and kiss that little girl for me.

Love,
your grandmother

Gillian refolded the letter and put it, along with the pamphlet, into her top dresser drawer. As if she planned ever to have anything to do with boys. Well, she didn't.

The next day, she wrote a quick note to Antoine.

Dear Antoine,
I hope you like college. We miss you. This is a present from my grandmother.
Love, Gillian

She got a brown mailing envelope from Aunt Corinne, stuck in both her note and the present, and addressed it. She got Uncle Henry to drive her to the post office.

"It's a present for my cousin," she told the postal clerk who weighed and insured it.

13

Uncle Henry

DAYS AND WEEKS after Antoine had left, long after school had started, Gillian was following Uncle Henry around wherever he went—beside him every evening watching television news, weekends with him in his basement workshop; when he took the car to get it washed or put gasoline in it; occasionally, where government security badges were involved, waiting by herself in the front passenger seat for Uncle Henry to do what he had to and get back.

"It does my heart good to see how they're bonding," Aunt Corinne told her sister, Antoine's mother, on the telephone. "At least I don't have to bite my tongue anymore to keep from telling her what to put on. She's stopped expressing herself by what she's not wearing. She's also stopped filling DeeDee's head with all those gory bedtime stories."

DeeDee, however, missed them, and not just the stories. She missed Gillian's attention, too, and her father's. It isn't fair, DeeDee thought; then sometimes threw tantrums.

And what did Uncle Henry think? Probably, on the one hand, thought DeeDee was too old to start having tantrums. Probably, on the other hand, was relieved to see his only niece showing signs of adjustment. One thing you could say for Gillian, and Uncle Henry often did, she was easy to have around. Didn't chatter all the time, or complain, or ask him questions every minute. Not that she didn't have some. Answers, in fact, were her main reason for running along behind Uncle Henry now. Untalkative as he generally was, though, Gillian had no idea where to start. So she waited, bided her time, hoped the right situation would present itself. What if it doesn't? Then a person can just forget it or else take a deep breath and plunge in. Gillian plunged.

"I heard about what happened to your mother," she said one Saturday morning when she was with Uncle Henry in his basement workshop, watching as he put together some old clock. "Antoine told me."

"Yes?" said her uncle.

"About her shooting your stepfather."

"I see." Uncle Henry held up a clock part in one hand, scrutinized it through a magnifying lens. Gillian almost let the subject go, but instead she rushed ahead, filling in the details—about the blood, the finger paint, the police, the asylum, the foster homes— until she ran out of words, or stopped herself.

"Is it true?" she asked finally. Uncle Henry set down his lens, put down his clock part, sighed, and sat back. He looked at Gillian for a long half minute.

"Pretty near true. It's about how it happened." He stood. "Tell you what—I have errands to run. Why don't you come with me? We'll talk on the way." But they didn't. Before Uncle Henry talked, he liked planning ahead what to say. He made several stops without conversation; bought wood chips for the lawn at the supermarket, faucet washers at the hardware store, then on to A & W for paper supplies. By the time he drove to the pond where the swans swam, near the lab, and parked, I'd say he felt about as ready as he ever would to discuss his childhood. He got out, removed a blanket from the car trunk, laid it down.

"Have a seat," he told Gillian, and began:

"I don't know why Antoine told you what he did, but I'm sure he had reasons. You probably already know his own early life wasn't easy. But he got by it. The same as me. So we can see it's possible. I think the main thing is not to dwell on what's past. My own opinion, which I don't expect the world to share, is we all can find something in our lives that will drive us crazy if we let it. I don't plan to let it. I advise you not to let it either. We're not responsible for what other people have done, however much we may love them. One of the last things my mother said, before they took her away, was, 'I messed up my life, Henry. Don't you do yours that way. You be a good boy, and look out for Paulie.' I was only nine, but Lord knows, I tried."

"You called my father Paulie?" It was the first Gillian had heard of his nickname. "What was he like?"

Uncle Henry's face softened. "He was adorable. It could break your heart to look at him. He was tall for his age, had long legs like you, and was always very thin. Very, very pale, too. He had wild curly hair, part blond and part reddish; and eyes like yours, only gray.

"Sometimes he wheezed and had trouble breathing, because of asthma. He had trouble sleeping, too, on account of nightmares. He'd sit up in bed in the middle of the night, too scared to move, shaking. 'Henry,' he'd whisper. I'd get up from my bed and climb into his. Both of us were usually wet in the morning. We'd have to rinse everything out—sheets, pajamas, underwear—and hang it all up; everyone would see. That was in the home. I still worry one night I'll need to use the bathroom, think it's a dream, and wet the bed. What would Aunt Corinne say?" Uncle Henry smiled. He didn't look worried.

"So then what happened?" Gillian asked.

"So then we grew up."

"Antoine said you always kept a positive attitude. He said I should, too."

"It's not bad advice," said her uncle. "But I didn't always. For instance, when your father dropped out of school and married your mom, I didn't have a positive attitude. I was furious."

"On account of Mom's being black?" Gillian asked, her tone half-surprised, half-belligerent. Possibly, too, she even felt glad, for a single hot moment, finally to have such a good, clear-cut reason to go with her anger—low-grade, nonspecific, constant inside her.

"Not at all. What did I care about that?" said Uncle Henry. "I blamed her for your father's dropping out of school. 'Throwing away his life,' I called it, knowing he'd be drafted. Well, I was right about that; he was and he did. But I was wrong blaming your mom. It wasn't her fault. I was probably also jealous, saw your mom as coming between us. 'Look out for Paulie,' my mom had said, and I'd spent my whole life doing that. Even to the point of getting just a two-year degree for myself so I could put money aside for your father's tuition. And for what? Now he didn't need it or me; and, I guess, without him to look out for, I'd lost the focus of my life." Uncle Henry sighed.

"It seems too much of anything, even supervision,

can be bad for a person. I believe it made your father lack confidence in himself. That's what I think he was doing—trying to prove he didn't need me or anyone. 'So what are you doing leaning on drugs?' I once asked him. But it was already too late." Gillian felt her heart flinch, so bitter was her uncle's tone.

"You can only look out for a person so far. Even someone you love, you can't save from everything." Uncle Henry unclenched the fists he'd made while speaking.

"Grandma tries to save me. That's why she sent me to Tennessee, to protect me, she said."

Uncle Henry smiled. "Just because you can't protect anyone from everything doesn't mean you can't protect someone from some things. The main thing, I suppose, is there's no saving those who are bound and determined on destroying themselves."

"Is that what you think my father was?"

"What do you think?" Uncle Henry asked. "Is there someone in this world who doesn't know what drugs will do to you when you take them? I was so angry at your father when he died, I didn't know what to do with myself. I've learned since not to dwell on it. A person can stay angry or get on with his life, but not both."

"So what did you do?"

"I got lucky, maybe for the first time in my life. I met your aunt Corinne." Anyone knows what comes next. They fell in love and got married. Uncle Henry had someone new to look out for and take care of, someone who needed him and loved him, again. He could be happy. Well, that's what surprised me! What Uncle Henry told Gillian was, "The main thing your aunt Corinne taught me was what my mother left out—take care of yourself. See, it's not enough just to look out for someone else. You also have to care about your own self. I saw my brother make that mistake. Aunt Corinne wasn't about to let me, at least not if we were going to have a relationship. She encouraged me to reexamine my life, seek out new directions. I went back to school, got my engineering degree, which your father didn't, wouldn't, hadn't seen the need for. You could say I turned my life around. Along the way, I married Aunt Corinne, and we had DeeDee."

"And everyone lived happily ever after." Gillian's smile was bittersweet.

"Of course not," said Uncle Henry. "That's only in a fairy tale. Real life has its ups and downs. Aunt Corinne says the best way to get through it is to look at it as an adventure. I'm sure that's good advice, but easier for some than others. Aunt Corinne, for instance, lacks our experience. She grew up in a very ordinary family in a small Iowa town, with one older sister she loved and two reliable parents. I'd say her marrying me was the riskiest thing she'd ever done. And, see, even that turned out fine."

Gillian sat quietly, then smiled to herself. Finally, she thought, a love story in which nothing bad happens. Well, Aunt Corinne did know from the start all about her future husband, including his relatives. Gillian wondered, for the first time, how much her own mother had known about Gillian's father, and when. Gillian shrugged. This was all very interesting to consider, but she had something more pressing on her mind.

"Can I ask you another question?"

"Now's your chance," said her uncle.

"Antoine said that at the time of the shooting, you were doing homework, and my father was finger-painting. What I want to know is, was my father artistic? I mean, did he like drawing and stuff?" I'd say what she really wanted to know was, did she take after her father in this way. Was that what so many cigarette holes were about this past summer? And, if yes, then in how many other ways, and was she destined to follow in his footsteps? It's tricky trying to interpret a child's state of mind; yet, if you love that child, you had better try. Uncle Henry sat still a minute or two, thinking.

"Where we were, there weren't a whole lot of art materials to work with," he finally said. "I guess he drew some. He also liked stories, the same as you and DeeDee. He used to pester me to tell him some. If you're interested, I'll tell you one. I heard it at work from Dr. Li. She heard it from her mother."

"I'm interested," said Gillian. Her uncle began:

"Once upon a time, someone was walking alongside a riverbank, when he saw a man about to throw a child into the water. The child was screaming in terror.

" 'What are you doing? Why are you throwing that child into the river?' asked the passerby.

" 'No problem,' came the answer. 'Her father is a first-rate swimmer.' "

Uncle Henry wanted to be sure Gillian got the point. "You see, it doesn't follow, just because the father swims, the child knows how," he said. "Of course, it also doesn't mean the child will drown. The point is, knowing something about a person's relatives doesn't mean you can predict a thing about that person."

"So what does it mean?" Gillian asked. Uncle Henry thought a minute.

"It probably means it's time we signed you up for swimming lessons." He stood as he spoke, got ready to leave. Gillian stood, too, but in her mind knew they still had at least one piece of unfinished business.

"Do you think my father was the one who gave my mom AIDS?" she asked on the drive home. Uncle

Henry tried not to show how surprised he was by this question.

"Oh, no, I'd say definitely not," he answered.

"Why?" Gillian asked.

"Because it's highly unlikely he had it. AIDS had barely started then; and, also, when he died, there was an autopsy. It's the law in such cases. Drugs were all they found wrong in his system. I'm sorry, but I thought you knew."

"Oh," said Gillian, and wondered the rest of the way home why no one had ever thought to tell her that.

"MAIL CALL," Aunt Corinne announced when they arrived, and handed Gillian two letters. One was from Antoine, the other from her grandmother. Both were the usual kind—hi, how are you, I'm fine—but still nice to get. There was also a telephone message.

"Lily called. She said she was checking up on you now that you're back in school. I told her you'd give her a call when you got in."

"Thank you," Gillian told her aunt.

"Thank you, thank you, thank you," mimicked DeeDee, her tone out of all proportion to the circumstances. "Why is everything around here always for Gillian? Antoine's *my* cousin. How come he didn't write me? How come no one cares how I feel? I might as well be the stepchild in this family." Saying it,

DeeDee kicked the chair rung, flung herself from the kitchen, and flounced off to her room, slamming the door behind her.

"What in the world's got into that child?" Aunt Corinne looked toward Uncle Henry, as if for an answer.

"I'm sure just a stage. Don't worry—she'll get over it."

Gillian hoped, for DeeDee's sake, soon. Gillian could still remember being seven herself, going everywhere, doing everything, with her mother and grandmother. Nothing bad had happened yet, and she had their undivided attention. Gillian wasn't surprised that DeeDee was cranky.

"I'd say it's normal behavior, given the circumstances," Gillian told Lily, and also explained in a letter to Antoine, after which he mailed DeeDee a postcard with a picture of the academy. DeeDee stopped sulking only for about as long as it took her to read it. What else to do? Gillian felt bad. Fortunately, there was school to divert her, not to mention a new librarian who told a different story every week.

"Want to hear about a magic ring?" Gillian asked DeeDee one evening.

"I don't care." DeeDee shrugged.

"Good. When you're in bed, I'll tell it to you. Be like old times. It's not gory," she added, seeing how Aunt Corinne was eyeing her funny. Not too much later, Gillian sat at the edge of DeeDee's bed. "Don't think I remember every word exactly either," she said, and began.

"AGES AGO, there was a king named Solomon who had a best friend named Beni. The king decided to play a joke on his friend, which wasn't too nice of him. It put Beni to considerable trouble for a whole year. What the king did was make up a story. He told Beni somewhere in the world there was a magic ring whose powers were such that when a glad man saw it, it made him sad; and when a sad man saw it, it made him glad. Oh, how the king wanted that ring. Beni promised to find it, and set out to look. He searched the whole world, but even the most famous jewelers said they'd never heard of such a ring, much less knew where a person could find it. Beni became sadder and sadder. 'I will pay anything for that ring,' he said wherever he went.

"Finally, when a year was up, he returned home. He was very depressed. Beni walked up and down the streets of Jerusalem. He found himself in a poor part of town, and he stopped before a small house on a plain street. A young Arab girl sat out front, arranging inexpensive trinkets for sale. Well, what could he lose just by asking? 'I'm looking for a magic ring,' Beni told the girl. 'I will pay anything for it. Its powers are such that when a glad man looks at it, it makes him sad; and when a sad man looks at it, it makes him glad. Do you know where I can find such a ring?'

"The girl shook her head. But her grandmother, who was sitting in the doorway, overheard, and, beckoning the girl to her, whispered in her ear. The girl returned. 'Wait,' she said softly. 'We can help you.' She removed from her basket a plain gold ring, the sort used for weddings, and with a sharp tool engraved some words inside the band. She held it out.

"Beni took it in his hand, examined it closely, and read the inscription. Then he laughed out loud. 'Yes,' he said. 'This is the ring.' He gave the girl all the money in his purse and promised her much more if she would come that night to the palace door. Then he hurried off to present the ring to King Solomon.

"Well, the king had only made up the story as a joke. You can imagine his surprise to be given such a present. 'A magic ring?' he said, laughing, and held it up so he could look at it carefully. How fast his joy faded. He grew silent and thoughtful. Such was the power of the ring, for engraved inside its band were these four words: THIS TOO SHALL PASS. Of course, they were in Aramaic, which was what the king, and everyone, read. Now King Solomon was reminded that all the glory, and riches, and splendor of his kingdom were only for a little while. Everything in life is temporary."

"See," Gillian said, and broke the storytelling mood. "Life is like that. There's nothing so good, or so bad, it goes on forever. You have to look at life as an adventure." DeeDee's eyebrows went up.

"That's what my mom says," she told Gillian.

"See, moms can be right. I have something for you. Don't go away. I'll be right back." Gillian left. When she returned, she was carrying the pink stone she usually kept on her bookcase.

"Here, it's for you. It's a present." She handed it to DeeDee.

"Thank you. What's it for?" DeeDee asked. Naturally, she'd seen it before, and knew Gillian had brought it with her from New York.

"It's a rose quartz stone from the Islands. It's supposed to be lucky, but that's only superstition. It's been in our family a long time. You could call it an heirloom," Gillian told her. "I stole it from my great-great-aunt Sylvia when I wasn't much older than you. 'No, you keep it,' Aunt Sylvia said when she found out. 'I'm too old to need so much luck.' But for weeks afterward, my mother and grandmother told me stories about girls who were thieves and the terrible things that befell them: couldn't hear, couldn't see, couldn't speak. Everyone was glad, including their mothers, because now they also couldn't steal anymore. I had bad dreams for weeks. Anyway, one thing's turned out lucky—getting such a nice cousin as you. And Antoine, too."

"Mommie says, don't steal because you don't want to be a thief," DeeDee told her. Gillian tucked DeeDee's blanket around her.

"It's good advice." She bent down and kissed DeeDee on her forehead. *Never kiss a baby on the mouth. It spreads germs,* Gillian's mother and grandmother used to warn her.

"Gillian?" DeeDee plucked at Gillian's sleeve.

"Yes?"

"I love you. I'm sorry I've been so mean lately." How grown-up she sounded. Gillian bent lower. She put her lips against DeeDee's and kissed her.

"I love you, too. Pleasant dreams, and sleep tight." Gillian turned out the light. Then she realized she'd been sleeping pretty well herself, lately. Not always pleasant dreams, but at least no more shivering nightmares, or hardly ever. She hummed to herself as she went along the hallway. Sitting in the living room, Aunt Corinne heard her.

"I wonder what's got into Gillian? She seems much happier, doesn't she?" She looked at Uncle Henry. "So, what do the two of you find to talk so much about anyway? All that time by yourselves." She didn't consider herself prying. She was only trying to find out. I'd say she was probably also going through a period of adjustment herself.

"Oh, this and that," Uncle Henry said, smiling. "Just things."

14

More Letters

THROUGH THE YEARS, I've kept close tabs on Gillian, though not always through letters. Whole months went by right after her mother died when I hardly heard from her. I often spoke with her grandmother. "How's Gillian doing?" I asked every time. Then, when autumn came, Gillian's correspondence picked up. Dear Ms. Ramos, she wrote . . .

❧   ❧   ❧

September

———————,

I'm sorry I haven't written in a while. Grandma says whenever she speaks with you, you ask about me. Thank you, and thank you also for all the cards and packages you've sent. You are a very good cookie baker. DeeDee thinks so, too. I use the granite rock from Central Park as a paperweight. It comes in especially handy, as I gave DeeDee my rose quartz Island stone. Please forgive my being such a bad letter writer this year. A lot has been going on, and I am sure you will be glad to hear I am working at adjusting.

I am in eighth grade this year, and so far, so good. I am in mostly honors classes, based on tests we took last spring. I have math with Julianne, whom you may recall from the time of the wild mushrooms. She has changed a lot since then, and I find her rather snooty now. Thank goodness for Valerie, who is my best friend in homeroom. We also have art class together.

I will write to you again soon, and I hope you write back to me. I like hearing from you about Grandma. Otherwise, I have only her word for how she is doing, and I know she doesn't like to worry me. I will feel better when I see her at Christmas. She's supposed to be coming here for a visit.

Take care,
Gillian

——————————— ,

Thank you for the beautiful pictures you sent from the Japanese appliqué show. I taped the red fish and the tan dog onto the wall in my room. Just looking at them there makes me feel happy. I took the rest into school to show Mr. Hanson, my art teacher. He liked them, too. "See, you have to work very hard to make something seem so easy," he told me.

Lately, I have been thinking about becoming an artist myself. Well, not all the time. Sometimes I have to think about other things, algebra, for example. Just when I thought I was getting the point, along came linear equations.

"Just hang in there. It was hard for me, too. If you keep at it, one day everything will suddenly come clear, and you'll wonder why it ever seemed confusing," Uncle Henry told me. I hope he is right.

"Don't worry, Gillian. Second grade is hard for me, too," DeeDee said. I have been helping her with addition and subtraction. I can remember second grade, but it seems such a long time ago. When I think back, it's as though it happened to some other person. I try not to think back, though, because it usually makes me feel sad.

Write soon.
Love,
Gillian

ॐ   ॐ   ॐ

October

_____ ,

    Thank you for your letter. I'd almost forgotten about Jewish holidays until you mentioned your office was closed on account of one. They don't have them here. Well, I'm sure they do, but nothing closes, not even the schools. No one was missing from class that I noticed. I miss all those nice fall days off. One interesting thing did happen, although it didn't have anything to do with the holidays.

    Two women came to speak at our school. One was a Holocaust survivor, and the other a rescuer. The rescuer came from Belgium. Now she lives with her family in New Jersey. During World War II, when Jewish people in Europe were being rounded up to be put into gas chambers, she and her mother hid Jewish children in their house and also gave out false identification papers and food ration cards to others. It was very dangerous. They could all have been killed if anyone had been caught. In one town, a whole family, including two babies, was hanged just for helping. The family they helped was hanged, too. But the woman who came to my class, and her mother, managed to rescue over thirty people during the war without getting caught. "Even so, I always think maybe I could have done more. Every night, I pray for the world to be better," she said.

The Jewish woman lives in Tennessee. She survived by hiding in a village in France. "Five thousand Jewish people were saved in that village. Not a single one was ever turned away," she told us. She said it goes to show what was possible. She said she had come to believe that goodness, the same as evil, could be contagious. Do you think she is right?

When I thought about it later, I thought about the Underground Railroad in this country to rescue Americans from slavery, and the people who risked their lives helping. I wonder if anyone knows more than one or two of their names. I think it's like the survivor told our class: "It's important to honor these brave people who risked their lives to rescue strangers. But it's important, too, to remember these people were hardly a drop in the ocean."

[176]

When I came home, I told Aunt Corinne what I'd heard. "Yes," she said. "I know. It was terrible." She brought home the diary of Anne Frank for me the next day. Of course, I'd already read it, in fourth grade. "Thank you," I told her. I know she means well, but she still drives me crazy.

Love,
Gillian

P.S. For your information, Columbus Day is not a school holiday in Tennessee either; and neither is Abraham Lincoln's birthday.

October

――――――――,

Something good has happened to me. At least, I hope it is good. Uncle Henry says I am very lucky to have been picked. What I was picked for is a special program at Oak Ridge National Laboratory, where Uncle Henry also works. Every Friday after lunch and on Saturday mornings, I am to go to the lab and work on a project with some scientist. Gary and Jo-anne, in my school, are going, too. Also, Lily told me Alphonse, Donny's younger brother, whom I know from the summer, was invited. He is very cute. How we all got picked was on account of aptitude tests last spring, and also teacher recommendations.

Julianne says she overheard some guys in math complaining the only reason I was asked had to do with the lab needing diversity, meaning because I'm black. When I told Lily, she said, "They asked you on account of you're smart. There're always gonna be jerks. You have to ignore them." I know she is right, and as Lily pointed out, "If Julianne is your friend, why would she even repeat such a story?" I have decided just to put it out of my head altogether. I will write and tell you what I do at the lab, when I find out.

Oh, yes. I almost forgot what else I wanted to tell you. Last night I saw a special on television about adoption. I thought about my cousin Antoine, whom I know you know about from Grandma. "Adolescence can be especially hard for adopted children," the narrator said. His specialty was what he kept calling "cross-cultural" adopting, meaning when parents are a different race from their children. "Often, such children feel out of place in both the society in which they were born and the one in which they were raised," he said.

All I could think was, it's a good thing Antoine

doesn't know that. Or Mr. Dixon. I found out the other day he was adopted—sort of adopted. His wasn't cross-cultural, but he was almost an adolescent. Lily told me when Mr. Dixon was eleven, his mother walked miles with him, across the county line, to give him away. She was too poor to feed him. "So what did he do?" I asked. "I guess he did chores for the lady who took him in," Lily told me. "He also went home every Christmas to visit his mom. One thing he says he never felt was deprived. He says he always knew his mom loved him; and after some time, he thinks, so did that lady." Anyway, I'd say for sure, if Mr. Dixon ever had special problems on account of adoption, he's over them now.

> Write soon.
> Love,
> Gillian

≈   ≈   ≈

November

————————,

Last time I wrote, I told you about the laboratory. So far, I have been only twice. The first time was for orientation. I was assigned to Dr. Li, the same one who once told Uncle Henry a story he later told me. It was about swimming. Now I see why. Dr. Li's specialty is ecology. She is trying to find out the effects of certain changes in the environment on fish; also on tomatoes. I'm supposed to be helping.

I'm glad I did not get Gary's assignment. He is assigned to the mouse house. If it has another, more scientific name, I don't know it. Mouse house is what everyone calls it. I have no idea what they do there, but my guess is, it's probably as bad as feeding birds at Aunt Corinne's raptor center. Gary doesn't mind. "Science is science," he says, which goes to show, as they say, it takes all kinds to make up the world.

What I forgot to tell you before is that something else good has happened to me. I tried out for the Christmas concert at school and got picked. I even have a solo part. It's very small, but as Valerie says, "It means everyone will clap just for you." Also, Mr. Hanson asked me to draw the picture for the concert program cover. I have not decided what to draw yet. If you have any suggestions, I would be glad to hear them.

DeeDee suggested Santa Claus. Aunt Corinne suggested a woman driving a sleigh through a forest would be nice. "It would be ecumenical," she said.

"Nonsexist, too." It turned out she was thinking of the poem by Robert Frost. DeeDee has a picture book of it. I went to look. Sure enough, Aunt Corinne was correct. Nowhere is it mentioned in the poem if the driver is a man or a woman. "But I have promises to keep. / And miles to go before I sleep," could be anybody talking to herself going home. What I think Aunt Corinne really likes about the book, though, are the drawings of owls.

"Thank you," I told them both. When I asked Uncle Henry his opinion, he said he had no idea. "I'm sure if you think about it, something will come to you." I hope he is right.

Last week was my third swimming lesson. Uncle Henry signed me up for ten classes. He drives me to the pool Saturdays after I finish at the lab. I am trying to look at it as an opportunity, and, who knows, one day it may actually save me from drowning. Say I'm in a plane that goes down, and my "flotation device" doesn't work. Personally, if I am going to be wet indoors, I'd rather it be in a bathtub or shower without all that chlorine. Also, judging by my first few lessons, I'm not cut out for water sports. To make matters worse, while I was practicing blowing bubbles in shallow water, a tiny baby was swimming by herself at the deep end. She kept leaping, shrieking happily, into the water, then swimming toward her father, climbing out, and doing it again. I think she wasn't even two. It's hard to explain how unnerving a person can find this. Anyway, I'll keep you posted on my progress.

Love,
Gillian

🐸 🐸 🐸

November

————————— ,

Thank you for remembering my birthday and for the beautiful earrings. We all went out to dinner that day. Aunt Corinne, Uncle Henry, and DeeDee gave me a pair of brass bookends that Aunt Corinne had made at the Art Center. Each is in the shape of an artist's palette. Even Antoine sent a card, the kind you design by yourself in the store. It has a picture of him wearing an aviator scarf and standing beside an airplane with propellers. DeeDee made me a collage card with an origami crane inside. "It means long life," she told me. "My teacher helped." I taped it to the wall alongside your red fish. "How does it feel being a teenager?" DeeDee asked. "Fine," I told her. But it's really a little scary. I'm not sure what to expect.

Grandma sent me this stationery I'm writing to you on, and a check so I could buy art materials. "Something special for your Christmas program drawing," she wrote. I bought more colored pencils, paper, pen points, and brushes, and best of all, a set of pastels. The colors are wonderful. Mr. Hanson offered to help me practice using them. They are very messy. I still haven't decided what to draw.

Up until now, all I have done at the lab is pick and count tomatoes. Next week, though, Dr. Li told me she would see about having someone start to teach me to draw pictures on a computer. Plus she's planning to take me into the field with her. "Fishing," she told me. She was making a joke, but not completely. It turns out that for her project, trout are taken out of Tennessee streams, studied in specially designed channels, and then put back where they came from. She is going to show me how to photograph them in their natural habitat, and also she said I might like trying to make an "artist's representation" of them. She meant a drawing. I hope we do this before it gets too cold.

Take care.
Love,
Gillian

[183]

&a; &a; &a;

November

————————— ,

    Thanksgiving has come and gone. At least this
year we had sweet potatoes and the turkey was fully
cooked. Aunt Corinne went so far as to make gravy
from scratch—mushroom gravy. It was only after
we sat down to eat that she remembered how I felt.
"Oh, Gillian, I'm so sorry," she said, and offered to
strain it.

    "No thank you," I told her. "I'm saving room
anyway for dessert." Dessert turned out to be
potato pie from Kroger's, which didn't taste
anything at all like Grandma's. Thanksgiving, in my
opinion, has always been an overrated holiday.
Even so, I hope yours was fine.

                Love,
                Gillian

❦ ❦ ❦

December

———————— ,

This is probably the last letter you'll get from me this year. That's because I'm so busy. Between school and the lab, plus the Christmas program, not to mention swimming, I hardly have time to breathe. I haven't gone running in ages.

Grandma is coming on the 21st, so she can hear me sing, then staying for Christmas. She said she has a surprise for me. I hope it means she's planning to take me back to New York by summer. It would be too hard to leave now, being in the middle of so many things, including the school year. I hope it doesn't mean she's planning to leave the country and go running, say in Zimbabwe.

My big news is my picture for the Christmas program is almost finished. The hardest part was deciding what to put in. The rest was easier. First, I made a large cardboard cutout of a Christmas tree and pasted it onto my paper. Then I cut and pasted paper ornaments. Most are of aquatic animals, the ones that usually get left out. I have a frog, for instance, and fish.

All around the tree are families with different

numbers of children and parents. A ladder leans against the tree, going up to heaven. My mom is there. I cut her face from a photo and pasted it on. She isn't alone, but I cut the others from magazines. Aunt Corinne suggested wings for people climbing the ladder. I think if there's a ladder, they wouldn't need wings. I do realize she's only trying to help. That's why I gave one person a pair. I also gave my mother an elephant to ride around on in heaven. In real life, she always wanted the chance. Now, in my picture, she has it. I put in other animals, too, including a zebra.

If you are wondering how so much could fit in one picture, it wasn't easy. "What are you doing?" Dr. Li asked the day she saw me making teeny tiny sketches of fish at the lab. "It's for the Christmas program drawing," I explained. "I want to get the right proportions, plus I need room at the top for my elephant."

"If I were you, I'd try using a larger sheet of paper," she said. So I am. When I'm all through, Dr. Li is going to get someone to photograph my drawing, then reduce it to just the right size. She telephoned Mr. Hanson to discuss her plan. "It's the least we can do for someone who's counted so many tomatoes," she told me. I still have to finish coloring everything in. I'm getting pretty good with pastels.

When I showed Uncle Henry my picture, he said, "Gillian, I think you left out something." "What?" I asked. I really meant, oh no I did not, because there isn't room for anything else. "You need to sign it. That's what artists do." I penciled my initials, GKH, in the lower right-hand corner, but a person would have to look hard to see them. My full name is already inside the program, for singing in the chorus. It has an asterisk beside it because of my solo. Valerie's has an asterisk, too, because she's concert mistress. It's too bad you're not coming with Grandma so you could hear us. Valerie plays the violin like a professional. Also, I think my singing shows signs of improvement.

One more thing I wanted to tell you—Alphonse, at the lab, invited me to the Christmas party at his church. It would be my first real date if I went, which I'm not. "My grandmother is coming that week," I told him. Also, yesterday, Dennis, in homeroom, wanted to know if I'd go roller skating with him over the holidays. I told him no, for the same reason. I didn't mention the only roller skating I've ever done was on New York sidewalks, wearing ball bearings clamped to my shoes. I still have a small scar on one knee from where the sidewalk stuck up with no warning.

Naturally, I didn't mention, either, my feelings

about going out with guys. Or getting AIDS. "Hey, guys are people, too, the same as us—just built funny," Lily says. "Trust me. I have three brothers. I know." I miss Lily. I only get to see her now and then, on weekends. We talk on the phone. It's true I have Valerie to talk to at school, but it isn't the same.

Love,
Gillian

P.S. Don't worry. I know a person can't get AIDS simply from dating. Plus I think no one I know here has it. I wish I knew for sure, though, how my mom got it. Uncle Henry says it wasn't from my father. "It's highly unlikely your father had it," he told me. But I think you can't ever be sure. Doctors don't know everything, especially about AIDS. I've discussed it with Lily. "My mom had boyfriends," I told her. She said, "We're not put on earth to judge our moms. The only thing you need to know about yours is that she loved you."

I don't know if I told you this before, but Lily is very religious. I have never even seen her eat a single thing without first saying grace. Anyway, her telling me that reminded me of Antoine and the memorial service he made for my mom. Where are you when I need you? I wrote him on a postcard. Although I was only joking, he called right away. "I'm fine," I told him, which I am. Well, I still miss Mom every day. But sometimes, when I think about her now, it makes me feel better instead of worse. Take care of yourself. If you see Grandma before I do, tell her I said hi.

GKH

P.P.S. In case you didn't notice, this is a very long letter.

‹‹ ‹‹ ‹‹

December

——————— ,

You are probably surprised to hear from me so soon after I said that you wouldn't. Yesterday was my last swimming class. I got a certificate. We all got certificates. There were five of us left in my class, out of the eight who started. My certificate was for making the most progress in the shortest time. If you could see the others in my class, you'd know I'm not boasting. Two are older than Grandma, and learning to swim for health reasons. The other two are DeeDee's age. One is a boy who's very chubby. His mother is hoping exercise will help. If it has, I can't tell. Chubby is not the worst thing for swimming, though, as fat people naturally float. Remember that tiny baby I wrote you about? She still comes to practice. Her father tried teaching her to float on her back, but she won't. She only likes diving and swimming on her stomach. There is nothing he can do about it.

I am almost ready for Christmas. I have just a few presents left to wrap. My picture is finished, and I could sing my solo in my sleep if I had to. Did I tell you it turns out Dr. Li knows all about the raptor center? "I admire your aunt's work," she told me. "She keeps very good records. They provide us with important information on wildlife trends in this area." I told her I admire Aunt Corinne's work, too—which is true. I didn't mention how I feel about helping her do it.

> Love,
> Gillian

꒰ꔷ   ꒰ꔷ   ꒰ꔷ   December

———————,

I think you must be tired of hearing from me by
now. Don't worry—this is only a Christmas card.
So, MERRY CHRISTMAS AND HAPPY NEW
YEAR! God bless you, and all of us. (The cutout
of the tree on the front is to give you an idea how
my concert program will look. I will send you a real
program when I have one.)

Love,
Gillian

P.S. Do you by any chance know what
Grandma's surprise for me is? I am hoping she
does not tell me she's getting married again. I
realize she meets more than just women in her
classes, not to mention out running. Not that I
don't want her to find happiness, but at least until I
start college, I want it to be with me. I'm crossing
my fingers for the next few days, until I find out.
She arrives Tuesday.

Love,
G.

15

Scenes from a Reunion

MONDAY EVENING.   Gillian's grandmother is in her living room, finishing packing. Even barefoot, dressed in a flowered muumuu, she looks elegant. The gold of her earrings and bangles gleams against her natural skin tones. Reggae music is playing in the background. Just for a moment she taps out the beat, with her dark-polished nails against a high bookshelf. She touches one hand to the small of her back and takes a deep breath, inhales the sweet fragrance of jasmine incense she's burning. She glances around the room, moves to straighten some photographs on her black lacquered breakfront. I remember when she bought it, used but in wonderful condition. Her daughter was still alive then, just barely. "Truly, I can't afford it," Gillian's grandmother said at the time.

"But I need something beautiful this minute in my living room."

The photographs she is straightening are a trio of portraits, arranged in a frame called a triptych: herself; her daughter in the middle; and Gillian, who may have been eight when the picture was taken. Her grandmother stares at all three of them briefly, then pulls back her hand. She measures their placement with her eyes. Her own, older, face is reflected in the mirror behind them. She sighs, or maybe I imagine it. Either way, it reminds me of a story, a folktale, told like this in Japan—almost like this.

AGES AGO, a mother left home and went to the village to purchase provisions. When she returned, she brought with her a beautiful silver hand mirror, a gift for her only daughter. Her daughter loved the mirror, kept it on her dresser, and took good care of it. Eventually, the girl grew up, married, and had a daughter herself. No long after, the mother fell ill and died at a young age. The grandmother retrieved the mirror and laid it in a trunk, where it stayed for many years. The granddaughter grew up in the very image of her mother.

One day, as she was helping her grandmother clean her house, the girl came across the mirror, removed it from the trunk, and looked into it. She could hardly believe what she saw. "Come quick," she cried out to her grandmother. "Here is Mother's face!" Well, of course it was really her own reflection the girl was seeing. Her grandmother looked and said nothing. Tears were streaming down her cheeks, and she was speechless.

But, then, I see I've picked the wrong story, because when Gillian's grandmother looks up, she's smiling. I think she's never looked more radiant. Is it because she's thinking of tomorrow, flying to Tennessee, looking forward to seeing Gillian and revealing her surprise? It worries me. I ask myself, will Gillian be happy when she hears it?

TUESDAY, KNOXVILLE AIRPORT. I can close my eyes, even now, and picture this scene: Gillian is standing at the assigned arrival gate, leaning against the wall-length window, staring out into the night, waiting for her grandmother's plane to come in. She's trying hard to appear composed, and from a distance she does. Not at all like DeeDee, who's almost jumping up and down beside her in excitement. Look closer, though, and it's clear how anxious Gillian really is, biting her lips, pulling at her cuticles, worrying over how much can go wrong in a week. Please don't let anything bad happen while Grandma is here. Don't let me make a mistake at the concert—trip on the stage, forget my lines. Let Grandma be proud of my drawing. Whatever her surprise is, let it be something I can live with.

As time ticks by, Gillian's fears take a new tack: What if Grandma changed her mind, missed the plane, isn't coming? The line is very fine between apprehension and anger: Why should I care if Grandma comes? Why should I care if she doesn't? She was the one who sent me away. But naturally Gillian cares, and deep down inside hasn't given up hoping: When Grandma sees me, she'll want me back. She'll know right away she made a mistake. Gillian takes hold of DeeDee's hand and squeezes. At the same moment, Gillian's grandmother's plane taxis up to the building and stops.

Gillian's grandmother isn't hard to spot as she exits along with a dozen or so other passengers, most of them men, most of them white. "Is that woman in the yellow cape your grandmother?" DeeDee asks. Gillian nods, watches silently as her grandmother walks to where an attendant stands beside luggage; picks out her own, a garment bag and carryon, then moves toward the building. "She's very pretty," DeeDee says. *Buoyant* is the word I'd choose to describe how she looks, her lilting stride, her upbeat tempo, the ease with which she moves, even wearing four-inch heels. Gillian nods again. I think how young she looks—and so vulnerable.

Then, just that quick, Gillian's grandmother is

through the entrance, enfolding Gillian in her arms, touching her face, her hair, patting her shoulders, as though she could make a year disappear just like that—evaporate in an instant. Well, she can't. They exchange formal kisses. Each takes a step backward. They stand at arm's length, their hands on each other's shoulders. They could be alone in the room, judging by their concentration. Passersby smile, seeing this serious-looking young girl who so definitely belongs to that grandmother; seeing that jubilant older woman who so definitely is related to that child. Or else they avert their eyes, unwilling to intrude on such perfect privacy. That's when a tear escapes Gillian's grandmother's eye, trickles down one cheek. Gillian moves to wipe it and feels a tear of her own slide down her face. Her grandmother moves to wipe it. Then, wet cheeked and tear streaked, both of them smile; the same smiles, at the same time.

"Just look at you, Gillian," her grandmother says, and I think again of that Japanese tale and realize this is where that mirror story belongs. Then the loudspeaker begins announcing new arrivals and departures. Uncle Henry moves closer to welcome Gillian's grandmother. He introduces Aunt Corinne and DeeDee, picks up the luggage, ushers them all out the exit to where the car is parked. They button their coats as they go. As they reach the car, Gillian's grandmother feels a tug at her sleeve and looks down.

"Excuse me," DeeDee says. "I know you're really my great-aunt, but would you mind if I called you Grandma?" DeeDee has no grandparents of her own. Her mother's mom died a few years back, and her mother's father died before that. "I still miss my parents," Aunt Corinne sometimes says.

"Mind?" Gillian's grandmother answers. "As much as Gillian's told me about you? Why, I'd be heartbroken if you didn't." She climbs into the backseat, moves to the middle, and rests one hand on each girl's lap.

"Fasten your seat belts. Ready for takeoff," Uncle Henry says from the front.

CHRISTMAS CONCERT.   If you've been to one, it isn't hard to picture another. The auditorium is filled. Gillian's family is halfway back in the center section, her grandmother on the aisle, then DeeDee and her parents. They all have programs in their laps. Gillian has taken her place onstage, behind the curtain, with the rest of the chorus. The orchestra is warming up.

"Gillian drew the picture for the cover. See, there are her initials. It was very hard. It took her a long time. I helped a little." As Gillian's grandmother admires the artwork, DeeDee goes on explaining. "There's Gillian's mom in heaven," she says, pointing.

"I see," says Gillian's grandmother. Tiny as the picture is, she'd know it anywhere. The pose is so familiar, and, also, she has at home a copy of that same snapshot, the one Gillian cut and pasted.

"Do you think that's us?" DeeDee asks, touching a family of five, three grown-ups and two children, standing by the tree.

"It could be," Gillian's grandmother answers. She smiles to herself as she traces with one finger their outline, drawn in pale lavender pencil. She looks closely at a fountain of colored water that decorates one edge, and sees a tiny baby swimming there among red and gold fish. "This is quite a drawing," Gillian's grandmother says.

Before anyone can say any more, the audience is asked to stand for the Pledge of Allegiance and the National Anthem. As the lights dim and everyone sits, Gillian's grandmother glances all around her, sees herself surrounded by a sea of whitefaces. I wonder if she's having second thoughts now, asking herself, did I do the right thing, sending Gillian here to cope all alone among strangers? But knowing her as I do, I'd guess not. Her eyes are on the stage now. She's probably thinking how fine Gillian looks, standing so poised and erect, as the curtain parts.

The concert proceeds without any mishap. Nobody trips or forgets a line. The orchestra plays mostly in tune. The audience can hardly contain its enthusiasm, not just with applause but also some whistles and bravos. There's a standing ovation at the end.

"Gillian, I'm so proud of you," her grandmother tells her in the lobby afterward. She admires her program again, tucks it carefully, unfolded, into her oversize pocketbook.

"I'm proud of Gillian, too," DeeDee says.

"We all are," says Aunt Corinne. Her rolled-up program sticks out from her coat pocket, where she put it for safekeeping. Uncle Henry claps Gillian on the shoulder.

"I'll go get the car," he says. Meanwhile, Valerie, Dennis, Julianne, and some others have stopped by to say hi and are introduced to Gillian's grandmother.

CHRISTMAS EVE, MIDNIGHT SERVICES IN KNOX-VILLE. Coming here was Gillian's grandmother's idea. Her daughter had most often sung in an Episcopal church. An Episcopal church was where her final service was held.

"Though I'm Catholic myself, I feel nearest her here," Gillian's grandmother is explaining to Aunt Corinne, as they find places all together along one pew. DeeDee looks beside herself with pleasure. She's thrilled being allowed to stay out so late. Also, she can hardly get over the decorations—such huge wreaths, so many poinsettias, the candlelight. She breathes in the wonderful fragrance of incense, admires the choir's red robes, starts feeling more comfortable, her family less conspicuous than usual, here among this congregation that isn't allwhite. She takes her cues from Gillian, sings, kneels, prays, stands, and sits. When everyone's invited to come forward for Communion, though, in her family only Gillian and her grandmother go. Gillian's grandmother has fasted since breakfast.

"I know it's not required anymore, but it makes me feel purer," she explained. She certainly looks pure; both she and Gillian do, simply dressed as they are in dark suits, so slender and solemn.

"This is my body. This is my blood." How soothing those words. Even just listening, a person can feel lifted, her spirits raised. Every good thing becomes possible.

Afterward, outside, Gillian takes DeeDee's hand. The night is clear; stars are out; the air is crisp, not cold.

"See, I did this for my mom." Gillian is barely whispering. "But I also did it for me."

CHRISTMAS MORNING. It's a homey, lazy scene. Everyone is up, but still in nightclothes and bathrobes. The tree is decorated with cookies, strung popcorn, old-fashioned ornaments. Some are handmade, and some, including the star at the top, come from Aunt Corinne's childhood. Alongside the tree, a folding table displays Christmas cards, including one from Antoine and his parents, sent from Hawaii. The floor is strewn with discarded gift wrap, tissue paper, opened boxes, clothing and books; an electric drill for Uncle Henry; a bonsai plant for Aunt Corinne; a set of watercolors for DeeDee, a gift to her from Gillian; a waffle iron.

"What *is* this?" Aunt Corinne asked when she opened it. "Oh, of course. Well, I've eaten them, but I've never actually made any." Fortunately, directions come inside, and recipes.

"I picked Gillian's muffler myself," DeeDee informs Grandma, cuddling up beside her in the armchair. "I knew that she'd like it, on account of it looks like a painting." It does, too, a modern painting, as though someone had splashed a box of poster colors on it artistically.

"Oh, I do," Gillian tells her. "Thank you. It's beautiful." Her eyes fill with pain, though. I think she's remembering last year, the red and gold afghan she'd bought with such hope for her mother.

"Please can I return this?" she had asked, even though she'd gotten it on sale months ago. "It's never been used. My mother died before I could give it to her." By then it was February.

"Oh, I'm so sorry. Of course you can."

Gillian shrugs now, shakes her head, as though dismissing what's tragic and past.

"It's just what I need," she tells DeeDee as she winds the pretty muffler all around her neck. "Look how it goes with my new running suit." The suit is a gift from her grandmother. Gillian's gift *to* her grandmother is propped against the far wall. It's her original oversize drawing for the Christmas program, sprayed to prevent the pastels from smudging. It is really spectacular. It's not hard to pick out children and teachers from Gillian's school, her friends from the auto body shop, her relatives. Even the baby in the fish pond looks familiar. She has on that same two-piece white and red polka-dot swimsuit the baby wears who swims at the pool.

"A baby can get an earache doing that," Gillian's grandmother tells DeeDee, who by now is sitting in her lap. They're both reexamining the picture from afar.

"I used to," DeeDee answers.

"You used to swim when you were a baby?" Gillian is astonished.

"I used to get earaches."

Aunt Corinne laughs, starts getting up. "Time to make breakfast," she says.

"Oh no you don't," Grandma says. "I'm making breakfast this morning. It's my Christmas gift to this family. Why else do you think I carried a waffle iron all the way here from New York in my carryon?" DeeDee follows her into the kitchen to help. It turns out a waffle iron wasn't all Grandma carried, and the air is soon filled with the wonderful smells of cardamom, orange rind, warm maple syrup, freshly ground cinnamon.

"When Gillian was DeeDee's age, there was nothing she liked to eat better than waffles," Grandma tells anyone, when they're all at the table. "Well, when Gillian's mom was little, she loved waffles, too."

"Really? I didn't know that," Gillian says.

"So, where are you planning to hang your picture?" Aunt Corinne asks. It's her way of making conversation. Gillian's grandmother seems to think this over.

"If you have room, I may leave it here for a while," she finally says. "It's a bit large to carry home on the plane." Gillian's face registers disappointment.

Seeing this, Aunt Corinne says brightly, "Oh, I know what we'll do. We'll wrap it carefully and send it to you by overnight mail."

"I don't think so," Grandma says. "When my plans are definite, I'll let you know." Four pairs of puzzled eyes stare at her. Does she mean let them know her plans, or what to do with the picture? Gillian frowns. Could this have something to do with her grandmother's surprise? And, if so, when is her grandmother planning to tell her?

LATE CHRISTMAS AFTERNOON. It's starting to get dark. Gillian and her grandmother are jogging on a level blacktop road that runs along one side of a lake. Wetlands are on the road's other side, and creeks radiate out at sharp angles from the soft shoulder. Gillian knows about this road from last summer, when she sometimes came here with Lily and the others to feed ducks, watch long-necked cranes soar playfully back and forth across water, and talk. There are no ducks or cranes today. They've probably gone farther south. Gone, too, are the blackfishermen Gillian saw here before, casting lines in the creeks; probably all home with their families, celebrating the holiday, watching TV.

"This is not a good place to run in summer. Motorists throw beer cans and bottles from car windows at joggers. I don't know why," Gillian tells her grandmother, as they slow their pace to a quick walk. Few cars go by, though, and those that do have their windows rolled up, and some drivers have already turned on their headlights. Aunt Corinne's car, which they borrowed to get here, is parked by the dock. They're almost back there now, strolling leisurely in blue running suits. Gillian's is her new one.

"I'm out of shape," they tell each other. "I haven't run since summer." Even so, by the time they reach the car, they're breathing easily. They pull up their jacket hoods and lean against the doors.

"So, Gillian, how are you getting along? I mean, how are you *really* doing?"

"Okay. I'm fine, thank you." Gillian's manners are intact. She gives the proper answer from her childhood.

"Good," says her grandmother. "I was sure you would manage. Now, I have something to ask you. What would you say if I were to tell you I'm thinking of moving here? Not right away. Say next summer."

"Moving here? With Uncle Henry and Aunt Corinne?" It's certainly a surprise. Maybe Gillian heard wrong? The house isn't *that* big, and, anyway, it's hard for her to picture.

"Not *with* them. Move to Knoxville. Take an apartment. The University of Tennessee has offered me a position. I was interviewed last month in New York. My appointment would be provisional. I finish my coursework this June. I can write my dissertation anywhere. Once I have my doctorate, I'll become an assistant professor. It's a good opportunity for me, and for the university. The main thing is, I would be near you. You could stay with me weekends, holidays, summer vacations, whenever you like. So could DeeDee."

"Why wouldn't I live with you?" Even as she asks it, Gillian sounds tentative. School is probably on her mind; friends she has made; Dr. Li at the lab, counting on Gillian's help next year. There's also a lifesaving course she's planning to take. Besides, what would she do without Lily?

"Aren't you listening?" her grandmother asks. What has Gillian missed? "I think the best thing right now is for you to stay put." Her grandmother goes on, explaining. "Teaching plus a dissertation won't leave me much time to look after you properly. And think how DeeDee would miss you. If you pick UT for college, you'll live with me then. Your tuition is waived so long as I'm on the faculty. It's a very good benefit. Also, there are two swimming pools on the campus, indoor and out. I'm counting on you to teach me."

"You don't know how to swim?" Gillian sounds incredulous. It reminds her of something, of someone. "How is Gigi-ma? And Aunt Sylvia?" Well, sure. Island children, both of them—water stories told of them, heading for New York.

"Okay. They're fine, thank you. Getting on in years, but then who isn't?" her grandmother answers. "Once I'm settled here, maybe they'll join me. So much crime in New York, drugs, too many homeless people; it's hard to believe, children carrying guns into school. I don't know what this world is coming to, and that's the truth."

Gillian raises an eyebrow, shrugs, moves her feet, trying to keep warm. My guess is she can hardly wait to get home, telephone Lily. "My grandmother is moving to Tennessee to be near me." Hardly wait to tell DeeDee the news. "I'm going to go on living here, but we can visit Grandma whenever we like." Hardly wait to inform her aunt and uncle. "It's definite. My grandmother's renting an apartment in Knoxville. She'll need my picture back as soon as she moves in so she can hang it in her living room."

ANTEPENULTIMATE SCENE.   Finally, some reason to use this word, "third from the end." Gillian and her grandmother are getting ready for bed.

"I've put the rollaway in Gillian's room for DeeDee. You take DeeDee's room for yourself," Aunt Corinne had said the first night. But Gillian's grandmother wouldn't hear of it.

"Oh, no. I haven't seen Gillian all year. It will be like old times." Of course not quite—or ever. Gillian's mom isn't here. And also, this night, the same as all week, Gillian's on her way down the hall to the bathroom to get undressed, put on her nightclothes. When did she become so modest? Her grandmother smiles. Thinks it's Gillian's age. Puberty is on her grandmother's mind.

"Here, this is for you." When Gillian comes back to the room, her grandmother hands her a package, rectangular—a brown paper bag, not a present. "I think you'll be needing them soon." It's a box of sanitary napkins, with wings glued to stay stuck to panties but that stick as readily to anything else. "Such choices, nowadays," her grandmother says. "Growing up used to be easier. Your mom started her periods when she was thirteen. That's when I started, too. The one I don't know about is Gigi-ma. In my day children were hardly told anything."

"Thank you," says Gillian, setting the bag on top of her dresser.

"GRANDMA?" Gillian says a few minutes later, already in bed.

"Yes?"

"Sometimes, I forget about Mom's being dead. I start having fun, enjoying myself. Then I remember. Right away, I feel awful. I start feeling guilty. I think I shouldn't feel fine when Mommie is dead."

"I know. I sometimes feel the same way," says her grandmother. "But we're alive, so we have to go on. Mommie wouldn't want us being sad all the time. Oh, Gillian, if your mom could just see you now, she'd be so proud. Well, I'm sure that she is. I'm very proud of you, too."

"Grandma?"

"Yes?"

"*I'm* proud of *you*. It's hard to believe—my grandmother a long-distance runner, about to get a Ph.D., become Dr. Williams, professor of sociology. Mommie would be proud, too. Well, I'm sure she is."

"Why, thank you, Gillian."

In almost no time, her grandmother's asleep. Gillian hears her snore and feels comforted. She stretches one arm across the narrow space between the beds, tucks her hand inside her grandmother's, and falls asleep herself. How peaceful they look.

KNOXVILLE AIRPORT, PUTTING GILLIAN'S GRAND-MOTHER ON THE PLANE TO NEW YORK. "Good-bye, good-bye," everyone says. They hug and they kiss. "See you soon." "Summer will be here before you know it." "I love you." "I love you." "Take care of yourself." "Stay healthy." "So long!" That's it; that's *almost* it. We could take leave of them now, just say "happily ever after." But, oh, how I hate leave-takings. Skip ahead, then, to fast forward, a series of pictures, perhaps a videocassette . . .

A ROLLER-SKATING RINK. Gillian has taken DeeDee; both of them have gone there with Lily some weekend in winter. The three girls are holding hands, frequently giggling. Lily is in the middle, trying to keep the trio on track, skating smoothly in circles and not straight ahead in the curves, crashing into the guardrails. For all I know, Dennis is here somewhere; maybe Alphonse, or Valerie, even Julianne. Perhaps someone new, someone Gillian hasn't met yet.

I look over my shoulder one more time. When you are *that* young, as they are, the whole world is possible—homes for the homeless, someday a cure for AIDS, eradication of illegal drugs and nuclear waste—anything. And any one of them may have a hand in bringing it about. But fortune-telling is risky—better leave now, tiptoe away, unheard above the din of roller rink music, the clacking sounds of so many skaters; go while everyone's occupied, content as they will likely ever be, and still healthy.

But leave, and go where? Who knows? Maybe fly to an island, or some other mainland. Maybe only cross the street. Anyplace with people to watch. Take up a new tale. Hold fast to the storyteller's certainty. . . .

There was a girl. I knew her well. . . .

Sources

The characters and events in this book are imagined. Some historical facts, and the folklore, have been drawn from the following sources.

CHAPTER 1
The story about burros that concludes this chapter is from the Caribbean. An authentic version, "The Two Donkeys," can be found in *The Magic Orange Tree and Other Haitian Folktales*, collected by Diane Wolkstein (New York: Alfred A. Knopf, 1978).

CHAPTER 3
The story that begins this chapter is based on East Indian folklore. "Two Sisters," a traditional version, can be found in *Folktales from India: A Selection of Oral Tales from Twenty-two Languages*, selected and edited by A. K. Ramanujan, Pantheon Fairy Tale and Folklore Library (New

York: Pantheon Books, 1991). Many variants exist in other parts of the world.

CHAPTER 6
The story opening this chapter, about the woman with no relatives and the serpent, is based on an East Indian folktale. An authentic version, "The Mother Serpent," is included in *Folktales Told Around the World*, edited by Richard M. Dorson (Chicago: University of Chicago Press, 1975). A wonderful retelling, "The Serpent Mother," appears in *Folktales from India*, selected and edited by A. K. Ramanujan (see Chapter 3 for complete citation).

CHAPTER 7
For historical information on Tennessee, in this chapter and elsewhere in the book, I relied principally on the following: *Blacks in Tennessee, 1791–1970*, by Lester C. Lamon (Knoxville: University of Tennessee Press, 1981); and *City Behind a Fence: Oak Ridge, Tennessee, 1942–1946*, by Charles W. Johnson and Charles O. Jackson (Knoxville: University of Tennessee Press, 1981). Also of interest was *These Are Our Voices: The Story of Oak Ridge, 1942–1970*, edited by James Overholt (Oak Ridge, Tennessee: Children's Museum of Oak Ridge, 1987).

The story about the trained carp that drowns is widely known, at least in the United States, and variously told.

CHAPTER 8
The autobiography that Gillian reads about a Chinese-American artist is *Paint the Yellow Tiger*, by Dong Kingman (New York: Sterling Publishing Co., 1991).

Chapter 10

For additional information on *bangungut*, or sudden unexpected death syndrome, see the *New York Times*, editorial page, June 7, 1981; and "Rolex," an essay by Diane Johnson, *Missouri Review*, Vol. XV, No. 3, 1992.

The story about the widow from Tamil is East Indian, adapted from "Tell It to the Walls," in *Folktales from India*, selected and edited by A. K. Ramanujan (see Chapter 3 for complete citation).

The children's stories in Gillian's after-school club are all true and were related to the author. Also true is the story about Erin, reported in the *New York Times*, June 7, 1988. The television interview with a Belfast nurse was broadcast on the "MacNeil-Lehrer News Hour" sometime in 1993.

The story about Lady Mary is a traditional English folktale, widely collected. My favorite version, "Mr. Fox," is in *English Fairy Tales*, compiled and annotated by Joseph Jacobs (London: The Bodley Head, 1968; first published in 1890).

Chapter 11

The story from Singapore is based on a similar story in *The Scent of the Gods*, by Fiona Cheong (New York: W. W. Norton & Co., 1991).

Chapter 13

Uncle Henry's story about swimming is a popular, widely collected Chinese folktale. One version, "The Son of a Good Swimmer," from the *Discourses of Lü Buwei*, can be found in *Ancient Chinese Fables*, translated by Yang Xianyl, Gladys Yang, et al. (Beijing: Foreign Language Press, 1981).

The story Gillian tells about the magic ring is based on Jewish folklore. An authentic version, "King Solomon's Ring," can be found in *Tales from the Wise Men of Israel*, retold from Talmudic sources by Judith Ish-Kishor (Philadelphia: J. B. Lippincott, 1962).

CHAPTER 14
The Holocaust survivor and rescuer are based on information in *Rescuers: Portraits of Moral Courage in the Holocaust*, by Gay Block and Malka Drucker (New York: Holmes & Meier Publishers, 1992). The French village where five thousand Jews were saved was Le Chambon-sur-Lignon. Details on the Belgian rescuers are based on Liliane Gaffney and her mother, Germaine Belinne.

The reference to the poem by Robert Frost with pictures is to the edition *Stopping by Woods on a Snowy Evening* by Robert Frost, illustrated by Susan Jeffers (New York: E. P. Dutton, 1978).

CHAPTER 15
The Japanese mirror story is well-known also in China and Korea. A version about a father and daughter was collected in *Chinese Ghouls and Goblins*, edited by G. Willoughby-Meade (London: Constable Publishers, 1924). It was recently reprinted in *Strange Things Sometimes Still Happen: Fairy Tales from around the World*, edited by Angela Carter (London: Faber and Faber, 1993).